MARK TOWSE

NATURE'S
PERFUME

ISBN: 978-1-68510-035-3 (sc)
ISBN: 978-1-68510-036-0 (ebook)
Library of Congress Catalog Number: 2022933847

First printing edition: March 11, 2022
Published by JournalStone Publishing in the United States of America.
Cover Design: Don Noble and Greg McCoy
Interior Photo by Florian Klauer on Unsplash
Edited by Sean Leonard
Proofreading and Cover/Interior Layout by Scarlett R. Algee

JournalStone Publishing
3205 Sassafras Trail
Carbondale, Illinois 62901

JournalStone books may be ordered through booksellers or by contacting:
JournalStone | www.journalstone.com

I am dedicating this novella to my mum, Jennifer Syder. In my short career to date, she has read close to everything I've put out there, enduring all sorts of dark and weird journeys. She's my first reader and editor, very reasonably priced (free), incredibly responsive, eagle-eyed, and I couldn't do it without her. Please note, there is an exclusive contract in place that restricts her from taking on work that isn't mine.

Love you, Mum x

NATURE'S
PERFUME

AS SHE RIPS the makeshift chain of wilting flowers from around her neck, she can hear her feet thumping on the ground but can't feel them. The forest is relentlessly sharp and unsympathetic as it swims around her in a fusion of dark greens and browns, but she sticks to her chosen path, staggering forward as fast as her aching body will permit. Voices emerge from behind and to the right.

Please, no more.

The days have all blurred into one, swimming in and out of consciousness, the only benchmark being food and water and when the villagers enter, full of liquor and ugly smiles. She's no idea how long she's been out here, but she knows the musty smell from the hut will be forever burned into her nostrils. They killed him, slaughtered him in front of her, gutting him like a pig, laughing while they were doing it. The ordeal feels like a long and horrendous nightmare, and that at any moment, she will wake up, back in bed in England, Matt lying next to her. She's spent too long hoping for that to happen, but out here, hope is all she has.

As the forest continues passing in monotone darkness, a snap of a twig to the right prompts her to inhale deeply and bite at her lip. She doesn't turn, just runs, internally chanting that everything will be okay. Head still cloudy, foggy from whatever they've been giving her, her body screaming at her to cease movement, the flash of brown between the trees offers a second wind. *The river!*

She took her chance this evening, most of the village gone, working at the twine around her legs and wrist, finally breaking free. Those faces, those leers. The things they do, evil, beyond what she thought existed in the real world, and things she'll never forget.

"Help!" she screams, forcing her way through the last of the heavy undergrowth, branches and sharp leaves cutting into her naked flesh. Laughter emerges from her left as she finally joins the riverbank, scrambling desperately towards what looks like the edge of a hut in the distance.

She knows she's lying to herself, that there'll be no rescue party. "Help," she cries again anyway, snapping her head towards the crackling forest carpet. There's no pain, just a silent force that sends her crumpling to the floor towards the edge of the river. Letting out a gasp as she hits the ground, she studies her distorted reflection in the water's murkiness, noting the stream of red running down the muddy bank. Something's scraping at her insides; she can feel it. She moves a hand down to her chest, running her fingers over the arrow that protrudes from her skin, feeling a flicker of relief the nightmare is finally drawing to a close.

Soft footsteps approach from behind, and she observes the shadow drawing in. There's a sigh as the silhouette contracts. Fingers run through her hair, hot breath falls across the back of her neck, the stench of tobacco filling her nostrils. "*Adios, mi amor.*"

There's a strong metallic taste at the back of her throat, and each breath becomes more agonising. The reflection in the water is fading, and the night's warmth is giving way to cold.

"We will miss you, but we have some new friends arriving soon."

*

Something scuttles across Tom's arm, but he isn't brave enough to move just yet. Burning an internal trail, a bolt of acid slowly works up his oesophagus, undramatically fizzing at the back of his throat and delivering a disproportionate amount of discomfort.

Today's the day.

He opens his eyes slowly to the generous amount of light seeping through the dirty and threadbare curtains, the pain instant and explosive across his forehead. The mustiness of the room and the unrelenting heat add to his growing nausea, his mouth feeling impossibly devoid of moisture. Noticing the hotel room door wide open, he quickly checks the floor, relieved to find their backpacks still leaning against the wall. Next to him, Loren lets out a moan and turns over, their naked, sweat-drenched bodies coming together once more, triggering a series of images from just a few hours ago.

It was supposed to be a tame one before the big hike, just a couple of beers in the local pub, but Nathan started throwing his money around, buying everyone drinks. It was a great evening to a point, full of singing, dancing, laughter, and the joy of being somewhere so far away from home. They were the centre of attention, and they let themselves get carried away. It started innocently enough, some of the older men and women who could speak a little English telling stunted tales of the Ecuadorian forest, fantastical stories about the magic of the flora, stories that were obviously reserved to charm the tourists and give them something to talk about back home. And what was that guy called that offered to be their guide? Jorge? He said he would take them to all the places they were bound to miss if they adhered to the track, but Nathan politely declined, stating he was a seasoned traveller and that the stars were his guide. Or some equivalent bullshit.

Music started soon after, and they moved on to shots—some vile green liquid Tom can still taste at the back of his throat. He grimaces, another bubble of heat and pain exploding at the back of his mouth. *That powder, though. What the hell was that?* Even though he only had a little, the rest of the evening becomes blurrier after that point, almost dream-like. But he remembers some of the men, even women, starting to get a bit too familiar, grouping around Loren and Isla, and that was enough for him to steal Loren away and stagger back to the room. A flashback of the door swinging open and Loren pushing him onto the bed fades as she turns over again.

"What time is it?" she utters.

Reaching across the table, he knocks off the beer bottle, spilling its contents onto the already heavily stained carpet. After a few attempts, his hand finally brushes against the sticky hardcover of the bible, and he coils his fingers around the phone on top, squinting to pre-empt the inevitable pain. "Just after nine."

"Shit."

As if on cue, a loud and extended honk fires through the window, and Nathan's unmistakably enthusiastic voice floats from below. "Rise and shine, campers!"

Loren groans. "Can you just smother me now? Make it quick."

"You know he's never going to give up. We'll feel better when we're out."

She pushes herself to her elbows, eyes half-open. "Liar. Pass me some water, please."

Tom eases himself from the discoloured mattress, his back providing a sharp stinging sensation as he bends over, digging the balls of his hand into his eyes. Waiting for the floaters to dissipate, he reaches under the bed, feeling his way across to one of the bottles of water. They found it to be the coolest place to store their consumables, but the plastic is still warm to the touch as he passes it to Loren, who quickly unscrews the cap and glugs down a couple of mouthfuls, eyes still sealed and spilling some of the liquid down her chin.

With a groan of effort, he pushes himself from the bed and approaches the open window, the breeze carrying more hot air across his skin. "It's stifling," he utters.

Loren offers another moan. "This was your idea."

"We'll be five minutes," Tom shouts down to the open-top jeep below.

"Come on, we're already losing exploring time," Nathan hollers in reply. Tom notices Isla has her oversized shades on, as still as a mannequin in the passenger seat.

He grabs the water from Loren, who still has her eyes screwed together, and washes a couple of tablets down, pouring the rest of the water over his face. "Christ, that man is relentless. How does he do it?"

"Practice," Loren replies. "I've seen him go all night, through to the morning and on to the next night. I tried to keep up in my younger days, but his tolerance is so much higher. Heavy fuel, he calls it. It will catch up to him one day though; take some consolation that—"

"What? What is it?" Tom says, noting her cheeks beginning to flush.

"Come here a second." She forces her eyes to open wider, still struggling against the light. "Oh Christ, that is so…"

"So what?"

"Embarrassing."

"What is?" He moves towards her, sunlight falling across his back, prompting another prickle of sharpness. Switching to camera mode on his phone, he holds it high and guides it across his neck, counting at least four bruises, one of them over two inches long. "The fuck? Was it a full moon last night?"

Her cheeks become even redder. "I don't think I've ever given anyone a hickey before."

"Well, you've made up for lost time. Christ, Loz, I feel about fifteen years old."

"I'm so sorry," she utters hoarsely, her voice no doubt suffering after all the singing and screaming. And there was so much laughter too; she recalls at one point hardly being able to see through her tears.

Tom continues to inspect his neck. "Do you remember much…about last night?"

"This morning, more like." She recalls the locals being so friendly, Nathan generously paying for a free bar. Some had very broken English, but others seemed well-practiced in chatting outside of their native tongue, impressively so. As the night went on, and as the drinks went down, and the drugs, the atmosphere changed, became tense, unpredictable, locals getting leerier and tobacco-stained fingers starting to brush against her more frequently. And then—

"Tom, turn around."

"Why?"

"Please."

His back is like an atlas, an abundance of red lines, some of which run from top to bottom, but others seeming more random and angular, almost out of place. Many are light scratches, but dried blood surrounds the more erratic ones. Near the top of his right shoulder blade, there's a pattern of what could be teeth marks. "Fuck, Tom. I'm so sorry," is all she can think to say.

Running his fingers over the raised skin, Tom looks across to her and smiles. "Do I need to get myself a silver bullet?"

Another honk from below finally prompts Loren out of bed. "I'm sorry, Tom, I—"

"Forget it," he replies, thrusting his arms through a fresh t-shirt, winking as his head stretches through the opening. "It makes me feel young again." He opens his backpack and runs his eyes quickly over the contents. They'll be back tonight, so there's no need to go overboard. "Is your pack good to go?"

"Pretty much. Just throw my lip balm in the pocket, would you?" She pulls the khaki shorts on and opens the bedside drawer, reaching for a clean shirt. "Why is it only the grubby hotels that have bibles next to the bed? It really creeps me out. Kind of like a last rites type of thing, you know?"

"Or is it more because such holiness threatens the evil sex demon within you?"

She rolls her eyes. "Come on, you know that isn't really me. Besides, you were a bit of animal yourself last night, what with all those little growls you were making."

"Get out of it!"

"I'm serious. Like a man possessed."

Taking one last look around the grubby room, they throw their backpacks over their shoulders and lock the door, making their way down the shabby corridor, yellowing walls and frayed carpet maintaining the grimy flow of the lacklustre hotel. The elevator is taped off and scrawled across a piece of cardboard taped to one of the doors are the words, '*no funciona.*'

They take the three flights of stairs down to the main but just as unimpressive foyer, and approaching the exit, near to the only fire extinguisher she's seen to date, Loren eyes the faded 'missing' poster, an American tourist called Chad Baker, all stubble and teeth. "Anyone passing by could have seen the show last night," she comments.

"If they had, they'd have called animal control."

Loren sighs. "Can we make a deal just to forget it, never mention it again?"

"What the fuck happened to you?" Nathan shouts as Tom pushes open the double doors to impossible brightness. "It's always the quiet ones, eh."

"Mosquito bites. Let's do this," Tom says, throwing his pack onto the back seat. "Morning, Isla."

"She's not quite human yet," Nathan comments. "Morning, Loren. Or should we call you by your vampire name?"

"Funny, Nath."

"Who's excited?" Nathan shouts as they pull away, setting off for the rainforest. The music kicks in, a guitar riff that Tom immediately recognises.

Isla moans loudly and tilts her head to the other side as if it will make a difference.

"You still playing?" Tom shouts.

"We're doing okay. We're not going to change the world, but it keeps things interesting while I'm doing all these bloody auditions."

"I thought you were going to work at your father's company?" Loren remarks. "Just until the acting warmed up a bit."

"I did, for one day, Loren, and that was enough. The old man drove me nuts! He's cut my money off now though, so I guess things will get a little serious when I get back. But hey, we're not here to talk about that. There's an adventure to be had."

Tom's hairs bristle on the back of his neck. Nathan has never let them down before, taking them out of their comfort zone, getting their heart rates going and adrenaline pumping. Last year it was white water rafting in New Zealand, and the year before that, cave diving in Mexico. But this year was Tom's choice, and Nathan's the man to get things organised.

"Quilotoa Lake was beautiful, but it will be nice to get away from people for a while," Loren says. "How long's the drive, Nath?"

"Thirty minutes tops. Not like yesterday. Relax, enjoy the music. There's a six-pack in the small cooler at your feet if you're thirsty."

The mere thought of more liquor makes Tom queasy.

"Jesus, what happened to you?" Isla finally says, lifting her sunglasses and twisting her face towards him.

"Blood-sucking mosquitos," Nathan answers for him. "Don't worry though; I've got spray."

"And how are you feeling this morning, Isla?" Loren asks.

"What do you think?"

Loren smiles. "Well, last time I saw you, you were dancing on the table with countless grubby dollar bills sticking out your pants. It's a good job that kid Jorge stepped in and calmed them down."

"I'm so embarrassed, I could cry," Isla mutters. "I've never taken drugs in my life. Never will again after last night."

"We left not long after you guys," Nathan says. "It was getting a touch rowdy, and Jorge recommended we disappear. I think the crowd was expecting a big finale. Isla passed out not long after; bless her."

The adrenaline is already beginning to kick in for Tom, the promise of abundant wildlife, some great walking, and a generous portion of the unknown. Enjoying the warm breeze cascading over his skin, he extends his right arm and begins moving it in a wave-like motion, something he used to do as a child when his dad took him to the mountains. Nostalgia often takes a bite on such trips, him and his dad more like brothers than father and son.

"I still remember that time your dad took us hiking as kids, Tom," Nathan says. "Do you remember, in the Lake District? What was the name of that mountain again?"

The coincidental question throws Tom. "Scafell Pike." He fondly recalls him and Nathan, legs going like the clappers, trying to keep up with his father.

"That's it! Scafell bloody Pike. It was so foggy that day, Loren. You could probably see, what, about twenty feet ahead, Tom? Scafell Pike was the only one we hadn't climbed, and it was the last day. Pissing it down, it was. Shit, we didn't even have waterproofs, drenched head to toe. One backpack between all three of us—a couple of half-filled water bottles and a bag of mixed nuts."

"Madness," Loren comments.

"It was all Tom could talk about the night before," Nathan continues. "Even though the news said the weather was going to be awful, he nagged at his dad all night for him to take us."

Tom laughs. "Remember meeting those three people on the approach, Nath? Fully waterproofed they were, Loren. All the gear. Huge backpacks strapped to their backs and trekking poles in each hand. They looked us up and down, all three of us wearing tracksuits and trainers, only a kiddie's backpack between us. They must have thought we were bloody idiots."

"Yeah, I remember! What did that fella say again? The one with the curly moustache?"

"'Don't go up there; it's a bloody death sentence,'" Tom says with an exaggerated posh accent.

"Idiots." Loren comments. "I'm guessing it's not the first time you've told this story?"

Nathan laughs and shakes his head. "I wish you had the chance to meet Brian, Loren. Top bloke! I miss him."

The lump at the back of Tom's throat makes itself at home, and the inevitable pressure behind his eyes prompts him to bite down on his lip. "Yeah, he surely was a character." Their closeness was something special, causing all sorts of complications for Tom's mum. When cancer finally took Brian, though, such memories were nourishment for their relationship, and he's closer to his mum now than he's ever been.

"I missed him by six months," Loren comments sadly. "Anyhow, did you end up going up Scafell Pike?"

"Your boyfriend wanted to," Nathan replies. "Got in a right strop when his dad said no. If it were down to Tom, we'd probably still be there now. There'd likely be a plaque dedicated to us. Here rest Brian, Tom, and Nathan—the bloody idiots."

"I still think we could have made it," Tom utters.

"Yeah, you're probably right, but not with your directions. I'll give you this; you can hike and climb, but when it comes to directions, you're hopeless. I'm surprised you found your way out of the womb."

"Ain't that the truth," Loren chirps in. "That's why I drive everywhere, Nath. Too much hassle otherwise."

"Where was that other place, Tom? That park in Scotland? Supposed to be a two-hour jaunt, but we ended up staying overnight, building a makeshift shelter out of twigs and fern. It was only by luck we bumped into those two people the next day. We looked at the map later to find Tom pretty much took us in two full circles."

"Stop it, Nath!" Loren sings, tears streaming down her face. "I'm suddenly not feeling like I'm in safe hands."

"No need to worry," Nathan says. "I'm in charge today. And when have I ever let you down?"

Tom sighs. "Jeez, guys, give a guy a break, will you? Besides, knowing where you're going all the time must get boring."

"Anyway, what have you got lined up for us?" Nathan asks, directing his glance towards Loren in the mirror. "It will be your turn next year."

"Haven't really thought about it," she replies, stroking Tom's arm. "Skiing maybe, or perhaps a four-wheel adventure—some serious off-roading."

"The latter sounds more appealing to me," Isla says, finally coming to life. "I hate the cold."

"It all depends on if I can get time off though," Loren adds. "It's a small firm, and we've taken on a shitload of work."

Nathan smiles and nods, knowing there's every possibility this will be their last trip together. He knows people naturally drift apart, even those that were at one time inseparable, but the imminent engagement and Loren's pre-emptive words leave a childlike sadness with him. He looks over to Isla, thinking she will also likely soon outgrow him and leave him behind. Her unwillingness to commit is a testament to that, but he knows it's his fault—chasing silly dreams, not taking anything seriously.

"That Jorge was a nice guy, Nath," Loren offers, sensing the dip in mood. "You don't think we should have taken him up on his offer?"

"Not my style," Nathan replies. "Surely you've figured that out by now."

Isla sighs. "Nathan's wing and prayer tours."

He straightens in his seat. "Hey, guys, I hate to repeat myself, but have I ever let you down before?"

"No," the three of them mutter in unison.

"Besides, I'm not a total fool. I studied the map, and Jorge gave me some tips; he told me that once we reach the river, we can use one of the communal boats to get across to their village. He said there's usually half a dozen tied up along the bank."

Loren wonders how he even remembers the conversation from last night, but his tolerance for drugs and alcohol has always been greater than hers. "And what if last night was just a drunken gesture?" she says. "What if we are left high and dry?"

"Worst case scenario, there's another village further down the river according to the map," Nathan retorts nonchalantly.

"And what if they're cannibals?" Loren says.

Tom's unable to contain a snort. "I think that might be slightly racist, Loz."

"Don't laugh too hard, Tom," Isla interjects. "I did a piece on that recently, about those five missionaries sacrificed on Palm Beach."

Loren adjusts in her chair and leans forward. "I remember you telling me about that, Isles."

"Yeah, that was a hell of an article to write," she continues. "The Auca tribe. Sparked quite a movement by all accounts though, so I don't think you have anything to worry about. Besides, that was over sixty years ago."

"Christ, this is like telling campfire stories." Nathan turns the stereo up and begins playing the air guitar. "Can't we just enjoy the music and relax?"

"Put your hands on the wheel, Nath," Loren commands, easing back into her seat.

"Guys, it's all under control," he says, doing as he's told. "Jorge said he'd give us a lift back using the dirt tracks if I promised to run another open bar."

Isla leans her head back again as if the weight of it is too much for her neck. "You trust him?"

Nathan shrugs. "Why not? He said if we weren't there by dusk, he'd come looking for us as that's when they get thirsty. But we should be there in four hours tops."

"What if we come across a jaguar?" Loren asks.

"Oh Christ, you're relentless," he rebukes. "You're a lawyer! How on earth did you get there being so god damned terrified of everything?"

"I'm fine with things I'm in control of!" she snaps.

"Chances are ridiculously slim," Isla consoles.

"And if we do," Nathan says, "take photos. Lots!" He flashes his signature smile in the mirror towards her. "As long as we don't try and steal its kill or challenge it to a wrestling match, it will leave us well alone. And besides, by the looks of Tom, we'll just let you loose on it."

"What the hell was that stuff last night anyway?" Tom says. "It's been a while since I smoked weed, but I don't remember it ever being that strong."

"Not sure, but it got my heart going," Nathan replies. "Made me feel as horny as a three-balled tomcat, and I've tried my fair share of stuff over the years."

Loren looks towards Tom, offering an embarrassed smile.

"Made me feel weird," Isla utters, bringing her sunglasses back down. "It was as though I wasn't in control. One minute I was aroused, and the next, I wanted to scratch everyone's leering eyes out, including yours, Nath."

Nathan lets out a snigger. "It's a good job that you're a lightweight and passed out then."

Tom puts his head against the rest, nostalgically resuming the slice of his hand through the warm air. "I've been looking forward to this all year," he says, watching the last of the urban sprawl disappearing behind them.

"Me too, friend," Nathan utters. "Me too. Who knows what will happen out there."

Tom responds to Nathan's exaggerated wink in the rearview mirror with a nod, subsequently running his fingers over the small box in his right pocket. The niggle of doubt rears its head again, but he knows there'll never be a better opportunity. Speaking to Loren's parents on the phone last week made him giddy, their reaction much better than expected, hardly able to contain their excitement, too, making him promise to take plenty of photos.

But what if? What if she uses her career as an excuse? They've just made her partner at the law firm, but all that means to Tom is that he gets to see her less. Even when they're together, she struggles to switch off. *And what if she doesn't think I'm good enough? A part-time waiter and struggling artist that's only sold a handful of paintings all year. What if I'm just a fill-in until someone better comes along? Fuck's sake, get a grip, Tom.*

He looks across to find her eyes closed and face relaxed, lips still offering the slight curvature of a smile. There's a fragility to Loren on these trips he rarely gets to see—out of the professional environment, free from strict routines. Her questions about tribes and jaguars added to the touching vulnerability, but he knows her better than anyone, and Christ, she's a formidable force. Nathan's the only fool she suffers, but he's a loveable idiot. In truth, he's never met anyone like her and still struggles to understand what she sees in him.

Finally caves to Isla's requests, Nathan turns off the music to a smattering of applause. "I won't take that personally," he mutters.

"So beautiful," Isla says, taking in the views that now surround them, enticingly vivid greens and browns begging to be explored. She can already hear the chatter of the forest, and floating in the air is a familiar scent, one that reminds her of her father's greenhouse in the midst of summer, an almost suffocating, but at the same time, sweet and spicy smell that is grounding and demands attention.

Loren's skin begins to prickle too. Hiking isn't her thing, but she's been feeding off Tom's excitement, and she's got a feeling about this trip, picking up on the exchanges between him and Nathan. She's played it out many times in her head but continues to manage her expectations just in case. "I read your piece on Puerto Rico last week, Isla," she comments, trying to distract herself again. "Really good stuff. More importantly, how is that book coming along?"

"Decent. I've probably got about four chapters to go, but I keep changing my mind about the ending. Thought I had it, but I'm not sure if it's final enough."

"No follow up, please," Nathan jumps in. "I hate sequels."

Loren leans in towards Isla as if to exclude Nathan from the conversation. "Can you give me any clues as to what it's about?"

She shakes her head. "I'll let you read it when I'm done. All I can tell you for now is that it contains beautiful scenery, gorgeous men, booze, and adventure."

"Inspired by true events," Nathan adds. "Me!"

"Hey, there's a shop over there," Tom says, tapping the headrest of the driver seat. "Last one now, according to the signs."

Loren turns towards him, eyebrows raised. He holds up his phone on the translator page, and she nods and smiles. "I was just about to be impressed."

"Plenty of time for that," Nathan says, prompting a fiery glare from Tom in the mirror.

"I'll pop in," Isla comments. "I need some mints or something to remove the taste of the God-awful radioactive drink from last night."

Tom nods. "Yeah, that was nasty. Almost fluorescent, too."

"God knows what they're into around here," Loren says. "Could have been liquified Amazonian frogs for all we know."

"I wondered why I felt a bit jumpy this morning," Nathan says.

To a chorus of moans, they roll up to the dilapidated shop, half the cracked window covered with faded posters of seemingly every cigarette brand under the sun.

Loren swings her door open. "I'll come in with you."

Stepping out of the jeep and performing an exaggerated stretch, Isla mouths a yawn. "Anything for you, Tom? Nathan?"

"All good," Tom replies.

"Pack of smokes, please," Nathan utters as he turns to face Tom. "You filled your hydration packs, yeah?"

"Of course. We're not amateurs, Nath."

He smiles. "Can you smell it? The scent of adventure. God, I love you guys!"

"Are you alright, Nath? You're laying it on thick today."

He glances over his shoulder and back at Tom, wide-eyed like a giddy child. "You're going to do it today, yeah?"

Tom shrugs. Doubt continues to eat at him from the inside. Perhaps she'll feel too much pressure to say yes in front of Isla and Nath. What if she feels different when they get home—when the reality kicks in that she's with someone that earns a fraction of her salary?

"If you don't do it soon, she'll get fed up with waiting!"

"I'm not sure people feel the same way about marriage anymore, Nath. But in answer to your question, yes, I plan on asking her today."

"Fucking A!"

The shop is as grimy on the inside as Isla suspected, the heavy smell of cigarette smoke adding to the oppressive staleness. She picks up the mints and takes the gum from Loren, keen to escape the claustrophobic dankness. Politely smiling at the old man tugging on a half-inch of cigarette, she walks over to the counter and places down more dollars than necessary. The man grunts and offers an almost toothless leer. On their way out, Isla eyes the poster on the notice board pinned underneath the picture of a lost dog. A young couple smiles back. Australian, according to the faded print, both about her age give or take a couple of years. She notices Loren glancing at it too, but neither of them says anything. As she exits the shop, a slight shudder runs down her spine, momentarily taking away some of the sting from the heat.

"Let's do this," Nathan says excitedly, opening the packet of cigarettes and slipping three into his pocket.

It isn't long before they leave the tarmac behind, the track changing to a rusty coloured dirt running underneath an ever-thickening canopy. "This is the road," Nathan affirms. "We're close." Crisp sounds of the forest filter through, and from somewhere, they hear the unmistakable screech of a monkey against the background of songbirds.

"That one's a howler," Nathan comments. "I've had a few girlfriends like that."

Unable to stifle a laugh, Tom pats his best friend on the shoulder. "Yes. Yes, you have, sir." He was scared to move this morning, but now he's giddy with anticipation, the scenery surrounding them magical and calling out to be explored. He's enjoyed hiking since he can remember— the smell of rotting wood, dying plants, new vegetation, and a multitude of other odours signifying life and death, but that somehow come together in an arousing earthiness that makes him feel glad to be alive. Nature's perfume, that's what his dad called it. This is his territory, his game, and he can't wait to step out of the jeep. As they draw further into the denseness of the forest, the noises around become even more abundant and sharper, an orchestral combination of familiar and new sounds that is at once haunting and exhilarating. Cicadas and frogs keep up the constant tempo, a reliable percussion spasmodically punctured by shorter and wilder riffs from the birds and monkeys hiding in the depths of the scenery.

Isla's eyes dart from one patch of the canopy to the next. "I'm actually getting excited now."

Nathan pulls them close to the edge of what is almost certainly a human-made opening. "Okay, this is as far as we go."

From the fauna to the right, there's an immediate and vigorous rustling that draws their attention, and, hearts racing with excitement, they quietly begin to exit the vehicle, holding their breath and hoping for a teaser of the main show. They stand in line, eyes pinned on the moving vegetation, Nathan finally letting out a sigh as the leaves begin to settle.

"Must have scared it off," Isla says. "How far is this river anyway?"

"Jorge said it was about a six-mile hike from here," Nathan replies.

She twists her face in disgust. "Six miles?"

"That's nothing," Nathan replies, flicking open his cigarette lighter with one hand and reaching into his pocket with the other.

"It's not nothing in the Amazon," Isla remarks. "How the hell are we going to find our way through there? It's Scafell fucking Pike all over again!"

Tom's unable to stifle a laugh at that comment.

"Trust me; I've done my research. You don't think I'd put all my trust in someone I hardly know, do you? What do you take me for?" Nathan says, slamming the jeep door. "Don't leave any valuables in the car, guys. Jorge's advice."

"Look, there's a sign." Loren marches across to the well-trodden opening. "Tom, what does it say?"

Nathan snaps Tom's phone from his hand before he can press a button and slips it into the side pocket of his backpack. "Quick question, guys. Have I ever let you down before?"

"We already answered that one," Loren comments.

"Just say it again. One more time."

"No, Nathan," they sing in chorus.

"Your phones; hand them over."

Isla puts her hands on her hips and begins shaking her head. "We're not kids, Nath!"

"Look, I just don't want everyone checking their messages and social media every five minutes. This is our time, time we'll never get back. We'll stop at intervals, take photographs, and whatever else you want to do, but let's pretend not to be tourists. Besides, if you have your eyes on a screen, you'll miss what this fucking place has to offer. Come on! All in agreement?"

Reluctantly, Isla hands her phone across, knowing all too well if they refused, he would stick his bottom lip out until he got his way. "This is an adventure, the group back together again," he pitches, feeling the pang of sadness again. "Who knows when we'll next get the chance?"

A rustle from the canopy above gets their attention, and they squint into the peppered sunlight, searching for the source. "You see, if we were sharper, we might have seen what that was."

"You're relentless," Loren comments, handing over her phone.

Nathan puts the phones away and claps his hands together, prompting more rustling sounds from the surrounding forest. He offers the group a smile and nods before beginning his march. "Come on then, let's do this, gang."

"Sometimes I feel like I'm in an episode of *Scooby-Doo*," Isla remarks.

"Wait, Nath," Loren calls. "The sign's pointing the other way."

"I'm not asking that question again. Trust me or go back to the jeep. Your call."

She turns to look at Tom, gives a matter-of-fact shake of her head and half a smile, and resignedly follows into the forest.

"You know it makes sense," Nathan mutters as he disappears into the trees.

"Impossible, isn't he?" Isla comments.

A sharp screech from above prompts Tom to snap his head towards the canopy. "You see anything?"

"Uh-uh." She arches her neck, searching the network of branches. "He's right about the phones. Plenty of time though, and I'm sure we'll get our fair share."

Finally, they follow their friends into the forest, eyes darting frantically, desperate not to miss a single encounter. It isn't long before the rewards come.

"My goodness, look!" Loren exclaims, fingers pointing towards the butterfly, its large cyan-coloured wings extending across the contrasting darkness of the leaf.

"Holy shit!" Nathan shouts as a squawk sounds above them. "Look at the colours of that parrot."

The group looks up to see the stunning spread of blues, reds, and yellows as the bird glides majestically overhead.

"It's a macaw," Isla adds. "We should see plenty today."

Loren's still cautious but no longer clenching her jaw. "Stunning."

Isla pats her on the shoulder. "And we've only just started."

They continue their slow walk, heads turning at the slightest of sounds, enraptured by the plant life brushing against them at almost every turn. Beautiful flowers emerge from the forest floor, lending colours impossible to define against an otherwise monotone landscape, giving the terrain an almost alien feel. They've been walking only for a few minutes, but Tom already feels his worries fading away, replaced with awe, wonder, drawn into the mystery his new surroundings offer. It's the perfect place, he thinks to himself. Magical.

"This is really something," Nathan utters from ahead. "I wish I knew what some of this stuff was called." He runs his fingers over a glossy red petal and leans in to inhale the comparatively bland scent.

"Oh, you mean like what a tour guide could have told us? Such a shame we didn't have the opportunity, isn't it?" Loren remarks.

"Can you believe those two used to date?" Isla whispers across to Tom as she marches ahead to catch them up.

Tom's thoughts are elsewhere as he eyes the hummingbird. It appears to be floating, guzzling nectar from the strangest looking plant he's ever seen, flowers standing at least ten feet high from the ground. He thrusts his hands into his pocket for his phone but, quickly remembering, lifts his head only to see Nathan's backpack bounding out of sight again. "Fuck's sake."

"Come on, Tom!" Loren shouts from ahead.

It's a hypnotic display, one he won't forget for some time. Focussing on the plant, he wonders how something so damn beautiful can grow and survive in such an environment, making a mental note to paint the picture when he returns, knowing full well he'll never be able to duplicate the same intensity.

"See ya, little buddy," he finally utters to the bird. *Shit. Which way?* Momentary panic ensues, his stomach tightening as he realises he's lost sight of his friends, indistinguishable denseness surrounding him. On the verge of calling out, relief washes over him as he hears Nathan's voice from ahead. "Doesn't it make you feel small? Some of these trees must be about fifty feet high."

Offering a nervous laugh at his little bout of dread, Tom ups his pace, almost immediately stumbling as something wraps around his foot. He tries to shift balance, but he already knows he's going down, his hands plunging into something warm and relatively moist on landing. "Fuck's sake." It isn't until he gets up and starts brushing himself down that the smell hits him, his stomach offering an instant churn as he brings the back of his hand to his nostrils.

"Come on, Tom," Loren shouts again.

"Coming," he says, wiping his hand against a large leaf, relieved nobody was around to witness the seasoned hiker's fall from grace. He catches up to the group, and they walk in silence, trying to navigate their way through the suffocating undergrowth as quietly as possible, each of their shirts now drenched in sweat.

Loren begins sniffing at the air, screwing her nose up. "What the hell is that smell?"

"We're in a forest," Tom comments. "What do you expect?"

Marching in silence for a while, savouring their freedom and admiring the trees that tower above them, they remain on high alert, tracking the sounds that float across from all directions. The forest has a hum, an aura, full of life that mostly remains hidden but occasionally teasing them with a flash of colour from above.

Isla gives Nathan a quick nudge with her elbow. "There, do you see it?" she whispers.

Following her finger, the group begins scanning the canopy above.

"Oh my goodness, so cute," Loren remarks.

"It's a capuchin," Isla confirms. "Look like monks, don't they?"

"I see it." Tom moves across next to Isla. "Hello, friend."

"Am I blind?" Nathan mutters, frowning and arching his neck into the sunlight.

The sound of fluttering wings captures Tom's attention, and he turns, eyes fixed on the huge bird that comes to rest in the neighbouring tree. "Holy fucking shit!"

"I see that," Nathan remarks. "Mother of God, what is that?"

"Oh, wow!" Isla comments. "A harpy eagle. I've only ever seen one before."

"It doesn't look very happy to me," Nathan offers. "It's a fucking beast."

"Harpy. Their wingspan can reach over six feet," Isla continues. "We're so lucky to see this. It's rare. Very rare."

Transfixed, the group watches it watching them, the stand-off continuing for a wonderful few seconds before it eventually takes off, its huge wings taking it well above the canopy until it disappears out of sight.

"Shit. We should have got a picture," Tom comments.

Nathan reaches a hand across to his friend's shoulder. "The eyes take all the pictures you need, Tom, and the brain is your memory card."

Tom shakes his head and smiles. "You need to write these down, Nath."

They continue surveying the canopy, searching for the birds that sing so sweetly, hoping the magnificent eagle will return. A few seconds pass, and Nathan breaks off again, already impatient and conscious they have lots of ground to cover. "Let's get to it, gang."

As Tom turns, his eyes pick up a blur of movement from between the trees they just came from. Instinctively, he leans forward, concentrating his gaze and holding his breath.

"You alright, Tom?" Isla utters as she passes.

"Thought I saw something." *Or someone.*

Loren joins his search. "Not a jaguar, I hope."

"Guys," Nathan whispers from ahead. "Come here. Quick!"

Tom is left on his own as the other two rush off, still adamant he saw something. Running his eyes over the scenery reveals nothing, but he's left suddenly feeling paranoid and quite exposed.

"Tom, come here!" Loren cries.

He maintains his stare for a few more seconds before heading off to join the group, glancing over his shoulder just in case.

"Squirrel monkey," Isla adds from behind. "Gorgeous, aren't they? That one's a male, I think."

"Look at the size of his tail," Loren adds.

"That's what she said," Nathan comments.

"Really, Nath?" Isla rebukes.

Tom studies the canopy, flicking his eyes over its denseness. "Shit, I see it. Hang on; there's two."

"Great choice, Tom," Nathan says, offering his friend a gentle pat on the back. "I wasn't sure at first, thought it might be a bit tame, but bravo; this is an absolute riot."

"Unbelievable," Loren says. "I can't quite believe we're here, Tom. It's perfect. A perfect choice."

Glancing around to approving nods and grins from Nathan and Isla, he knows the time is right. Hardly a drop of saliva in his mouth, he reaches into his pocket and wraps his fingers around the box. Nathan takes a couple of steps back, reaches for his phone, and points it towards Tom.

Loren breaks into a nervous smile, starting to eye each of them suspiciously. "What? What is it?"

Tom crouches to one knee, opening the box on the way down and holding it out towards her.

"Yes!" Loren shouts, instinctively clapping her hands together.

Isla lets out a guffaw. "You have to wait to be asked, Loz. I think that's the way it works."

"Sorry," she says, cheeks turning bright red.

Tom is smiling ear to ear. He winks at her and clears his throat. "Loren Dolphin, will you do me the honour of being my wife?"

Eyes watery, a single tear escaping down her right cheek, she nods profusely, sporting a smile so big it splits her face in two. "Yes," she says, much more softly than before. They embrace and kiss to the sounds of the Ecuadorian forest and cheers from their best friends. "I love you so much," she whispers into his ear.

Nathan joins the hug. "Congratulations, guys. You've got a good one there, Tom."

"I know," Tom replies, wiping the dampness away with the back of his hand.

"Come on in, Isla," Nathan shouts, eyes also glistening with moisture.

"Okay, but don't get any ideas."

"Yeah, I know. I'll eventually wear you down though."

They finally break and collect their backpacks. "Okay, back to serious adventuring," Nathan comments. "Let's leave the touchy-feely stuff until you get back to the room, though, agreed?"

Loren squeezes Tom's hand, and they release, falling back in line behind Nathan. Fucking A, Tom thinks to himself as the group continues on their way, snapping their heads towards every sound, carefully stepping over the ever-thickening undergrowth and large twisted roots of trees that rise from the ground like fossilised serpents.

Unable to wipe the smile from her face, Loren's skin crawls with excitement at the prospect of showing off the ring when they get home. "I can't wait to tell my parents. They'll love you, Tom."

"They already know. So does my mum." He winks. "I can feel my dad here with us too. God, he would have loved this, would have loved you."

"I'm really happy for you," Isla offers.

"Thanks, Isles." Loren lifts the ring for her to see.

"It's beautiful."

It's impossible to know how much time passes, even more so as the forest floor becomes darker, the canopy above closing in around them. They march at a decent pace, their journey pausing only occasionally and briefly each time Nathan hands phones across for the sake of taking photos, an event which becomes much less frequent as the landscape turns monotonous and uninteresting.

Isla leans over, angling her phone as she studies the almost colourless plant crawling with inch-long ants. "Are you sure we aren't lost?"

Eyes wide, hands on his hips, Nathan opens his mouth to speak.

"Don't say it," Tom jumps in.

"Have faith, people. When have I—"

"Don't," Tom offers again. "Just have us home for dinner, okay?"

Even with the huge backpack strapped around his shoulders, Nathan still manages to walk with a swagger as he forges ahead. Always has been a cocky bugger, and it's hard not to trust someone so self-assured. "The river is just up here; can't you smell it?" he says.

"He's a loveable prick, isn't he?" Isla says, tapping Tom on the back of the arm.

Tom inhales deeply, nose thrust towards the hidden sky.

Isla glances around and smiles. "You smell it too? The river?"

"I smell something," Tom says with a wink. "Wait up, Loren!"

The conversation becomes a little more stinted as the group continues marching, searching for a river that's supposed to split the forest in two. Nathan's pace is undoubtedly increasing, and Tom isn't sure to take that as a good sign or bad. "Keep up, guys," his friend shouts from twenty yards ahead.

"Oh, wow!" Isla exclaims suddenly. "Over there!"

The group turns to look to where she's pointing, stopping dead in their tracks, mesmerised by the majestic flower sprouting proudly from the random patch of dark soil. It's a magical display of rebellion in such a shaded and otherwise relatively lifeless area that is simply jaw-dropping. Half a dozen pods surround it, indicating that it's already past its prime, but contrarily, the strength of colours of the flower itself suggests perfection.

"I've never seen anything like it before," Isla comments.

Tom thinks it even more beautiful as he approaches the myriad of tentacles—deep reds and bright yellows exploding from the centre like an atomic bomb, circled by ten stark white petals that only serve to emphasise its internal beauty. He wants to paint it right now, capture the absurdity of nature and the alien-like form of the flower. He imagines each brush stroke in his head and the colours he would mix to bring the painting to life. As before, though, he knows his efforts would pale in comparison to the vibrancy on display.

Docilely hovering over its centre is what looks to be a wasp or a bee; it's nearly two inches long and adorned with stunning red and green pearlescent stripes that only complement the beauty of the flower. As the group draws closer, the buzzing becomes louder.

Isla breaks the silence. "Is it a passionflower?"

"I don't think so," Tom remarks. "But it's going to seed—dying."

"That smell!" Isla announces as she draws close to it.

"I smell it too." Nathan follows Isla in. "Fucking beautiful!"

Tom watches as Isla crouches, leaning in expectantly with eyes closed. As she draws ever closer, the buzzing of the insect intensifies, and it retreats a couple of inches as if to observe from a safe distance. A huge smile stretches across Isla's face as she inhales the flower, a perfectly beautiful epitome of life that causes her body to, in contrast, wilt to the ground.

"Careful of the bee," Loren utters.

"Could be a wasp," Tom suggests.

"Guys, you have to smell this," Isla murmurs, showing no signs of making room for anyone else. As she takes in another lungful of the flower's scent, her eyes appear to glaze over, and a strangle inaudible murmur leaves her lips. The insect buzzes in and out again, but Isla seems oblivious as she goes in for another sniff.

Gently placing his hands on her shoulders, Nathan leans her away. "My turn." He ducks in and snorts so loudly it prompts a laugh from Loren. "Be careful, Nathan. You'll suck the petals off with that thing," she says. The same vacant expression draws across his face as he lets out a garbled moan. He leans in again, getting even closer to the pistil, but before he even has a chance to inhale, the insect darts into his eye with an aggressive buzz.

"Ow, fucking ow!" he cries, thrusting himself up. "Fucking thing!" Hopping around manically, he waves his hands in front of his face, but the culprit shows no signs of moving, as though it's attached to him, its relentless buzzing feeling trapped inside his head. "Fucking hate wasps! Get rid of it." He reaches behind into his backpack, bringing out the large knife he's been boasting about for the last few weeks—top of the line and ridiculously expensive.

"Jesus Christ, Nathan. What the hell are you going to do with that?" Tom shouts.

"I don't know. Just get the fucking thing off, will you!"

Loren moves in, spraying the entire contents of her water bottle into Nathan's face, but the stubborn little fucker doesn't budge. Shifting from one foot to the next like an excited crow, Nathan lets out a high-pitched squeal that surprises them all. "Fuck. Fuck! Fuck!"

Sprawled across the floor, holding her belly, Isla alternates between guffaws of laughter and aggressive sniffs of the flower. "This is too much!"

"Stay still, Nathan, for God's sake!" Loren shouts, reaching for Nathan's eye.

"Get it off," he says through gritted teeth, knuckles white as he clasps the handle of the knife even more tightly. "Please!"

"Calm down." Loren moves her fingers towards his eye, carefully pinching the wings between her nails. Slowly, she draws it away, finally letting it fall to the floor, where it gives a few kicks at the air before death mercifully takes it.

"Little shit!" Nathan screams, bringing his boot down hard on its lifeless body.

"Wait. I think it's left its stinger in there." Loren delicately goes to remove the half-inch spike from his eyelid.

"Careful. Careful."

"I am. Keep still, will you?" Her fingers tremble, but she manages to pinch it between her nails, holding it out for Nathan to see with his good eye. "Told you it was a bee."

"Well, that was fucking horrible," Nathan says, nursing his eye. "Oh, and thanks for your help, Tom."

"Hey, man. It was just a bee, not a bloody pterodactyl. Besides, I didn't want to get near you while you were waving that monstrosity about. Are you trying to make up for something?"

"Your eye," Isla says, looking up from the ground towards Nathan, bursting into another fit of laughter. "Give him a patch and a parrot and call him Jack Sparrow."

"Fuck you, darling."

"It does look sore," Loren says. The lid is already turning a very bright red, the entire area beginning to swell, too. "Just don't touch it; you'll irritate it more."

"Can you see out of it?" Tom asks.

"No," he replies, wincing as he gently surveys the damage with his fingers.

"It's a good job that you can smell the river," Isla says between fits of giggles. "Because you won't be able to fucking see it!"

"Come on," Nathan says. "Let's get out of here."

Isla rolls back to the flower, taking a few urgent gulps of the surrounding air. "You go on; I'll catch up." Impatiently, Nathan coils his arms around her shoulders and hoists her up. "Hey!" she protests. But she's already back in line, as are they all—Nathan at the front and Tom trailing the rear.

On the way past, Loren swoops down and rips off the head of the flower. She breathes it in deeply and slips it behind her right ear, letting out a little giggle as she skips ahead. Behind her, Tom rips off one of the pods and slips it into his pocket, intending to visit Barbara at the garden nursery when he gets back, sure that she'll have some idea of its species, or at least able to offer an educated guess. Sometimes he visits for ideas of what to paint, but he can confidently say he's never seen anything quite like this, and he suspects she may not have, too. Got to be worth a shot, he thinks.

On the hunt for the promised river, the group continues marching forward, Isla wishing she could return to the small clearing and spend the rest of the day under the flower's spell, her body already craving another hit. It's all she can think about until the high finally begins to fade, and she once again becomes irritated by the relentless mosquitos and endless trudging through bland scenery.

Tom stops, raising a hand in the air. "Guys, can you hear that?"

Nathan turns, his left eye completely shut. "No."

"Exactly," Tom says. The songs of the birds and the chatter from the monkeys are undoubtedly growing distant. Even the reliable hum of the cicadas is faint.

"That's a good sign. Think about it, Tom. If we are close to the village, there's going to be less wildlife. Besides—"

"You can smell it," Tom interjects.

Nathan turns, urgently beginning to march into the thickness.

"I don't know," Loren comments. "I'm starting to get a little nervous."

"Me too," Tom utters. "But when have I ever let you down?" He mimics Nathan's cheesy grin.

The group faithfully follows Nathan as he continues moving forward, swiping at the ever-growing number of mosquitos and the thickening vegetation. Abundant knotted roots snake their way across the forest floor, making the ground more difficult to navigate, as do the low-hanging branches and vines from the surrounding trees that occasionally tangle up in their packs.

As if Nathan senses the despondency, he offers the group a quick glance over his shoulder. "Not much further."

In response, Loren turns to Tom and smiles. "Wait for it," she says, enjoying the scent of the flower as the hot breeze blows across.

But there's no punchline from Nathan as he comes to a standstill.

"What is it, Nath?" Isla shouts, sensing something wrong. She jogs towards him, stopping a few feet short. "Oh, Christ."

Loren and Tom also rush forward to see what has stopped their infallible leader in his tracks, Tom instinctively doubling over with a dry gag as the warm breeze brings the scene alive. The decimated carcass of the monkey is a mess of skin, bone, and intestines that glisten in the peppered rays of sun.

"Anyone hungry?" Nathan murmurs, lighting up a cigarette.

"Jaguar?" Loren comments.

"Turf war, I reckon," Tom says, brushing himself down. "Happens all the time."

"Tom's right. I've seen this before," Isla adds. "It's another squirrel monkey, I think. Hard to be completely sure, what with the head missing and tail gone."

Loren turns towards her, most of the colour drained from her face. "Why would the head be missing?"

A rustle to the right draws the group's attention, and with their breaths held, they follow the trail of moving foliage as it weaves a path around them, finally coming to a stop about twenty feet north. An eerie silence falls as they anxiously scan the leaves, unsure whether to hope for any further activity or not. "It could be anything," Isla finally whispers.

"Doesn't help," Loren whispers back, fingernails digging into her thigh.

They watch and wait for what feels like an eternity, no further chat, as still as statues as the warm breeze blows across. Eyes on the leaves, trying to distinguish if it's the wind moving them or the unidentified stalker, Tom suddenly feels responsible for the group, this being his idea, after all. His heart pounds, his skin crawls. He looks across to Loren, who doesn't even try and force a smile. Each year, their adventures become more daring, but to be stood in the middle of the rainforest, relying on vague directions from a stranger, armed only with a knife, seems almost implausible to him now.

As the breeze dies, the group remains frozen, eyes nervously scanning the forest carpet. They wait.

And wait some more.

"This is intense. One to remember," Nathan says, following with a nervous laugh.

Isla takes another anxious look around. "There are so many things it could have been," she mutters.

Tom unclenches his fists, stretching out his aching fingers. "It certainly got my heart going." Just ahead of him, Loren plucks the flower from behind her ear and inhales deeply. She lets out a little snigger and glances over her shoulder, offering him a smile and a wink, seemingly already over their little encounter. Tom feels smothered, though, as though the relentless humidity is wrapping around him and beginning to squeeze. There's an urgency to be home, showing off the ring to family and friends, away from the unknown and surrounded by mundanity once more.

"Onwards, friends," Nathan finally calls out.

Continuing to absorb them into its guts, the forest, once offering a sense of kinship with its flora, now only presents a harsh uniformity. The noticeable lack of colours and once abundant sounds fills them with a growing sense of trepidation.

"Nath, wait up," Isla calls, but he doesn't stop. She sighs to the others and jogs ahead, carefully darting between the now sharper undergrowth and stepping over the roots of the trees that appear more sinister, limbs aggressively coiling around each other, twisting back into themselves as if trying to return to the trunk for comfort. Finally catching up to him, she matches his stride, noting how clearly the sound of their footsteps can be heard over the distant soundtrack. Aside from Loren's mutterings of how much she adores the ring, this part of the forest seems unnaturally muted.

Nathan surveys the scenery ahead. It's as if this part of the forest is dying, and the further they walk, the less life they encounter. The trees are thicker, blacker, twisting more aggressively around each other, foliage now sparser and less rich in colour. Jorge described it like this, but here and now, it seems impossibly bleak and menacing. Plants are decorated with pale leaves sharp enough to cut, some even sporting serrated edges, as though vegetation has evolved to blend in with the harshness, entering into a mode of self-protection.

"We're not lost," Nathan finally says.

Isla studies his face. She's usually pretty good at catching a lie, and he certainly looks more agitated than before. It's been a while since he flashed the signature smile too. "Is the GPS still working?"

"It's too weak."

"Compass?"

"Vegetation's too dense."

"So, we're relying on your sense of smell and one good eye to lead us to a village full of strangers?"

"We've been heading north from the beginning. Trust me; I planned this route before we came," he says impatiently. "It might seem like I live life by the seat of my pants, but you know that's not true, Isles."

The lushness they were first presented with has given way to skeletal limbs struggling to perform their only job; a carpet of rotten leaves surrounding their base. She's been noticing it for a while, the sparseness of green above them, only patches decorating the canopy now.

She grabs his hand. "I trust you."

"Marry me then." As soon as the words leave his lips, Nathan senses the change in atmosphere, immediately wishing he could swallow them back.

She leaves go of his hand, letting out a sigh. "I knew it. I knew you were mad at me."

"I'm not mad, Isles. I just don't understand why we can't make a proper go of it. You know I adore you and—"

"Shit!" Isla says, brushing desperately at the imperceptible cobweb. "Why do we have to change things, Nath? If it works well, it just seems counter-intuitive."

"But I love you! I really do."

"You've seen how many have fallen already. All caught up in the fun of it until reality slaps them in the face. Dave and Anita were inseparable two years ago, and six months of marriage got them hating each other." She grits her teeth, raking her fingernails through dry hair. "And then there's Todd and Lucy. And look at my parents. Your parents, even. And what for? A piece of paper with both our names scrawled across it?"

"Jeez, you know how to take the romance out of things, Isles," Nathan says, shaking his head. "I want to spend the rest of my life with you, that's all. Suddenly, it feels like a crime."

"I love you, Nath. Can't we agree to differ on this and just live our lives? I thought we already did this?"

It's as though the words are like bile that he has to get rid of. Even before he mouths them, he knows how they'll be received. "Is it because I'm just a waiter? I'm going to get a break soon, Isles. I promise."

"Fuck off, Nath," she says, marching ahead. "You really think I'm that fucking shallow?"

Cursing himself for being so pathetic, he watches her angrily swiping at the vegetation, wishing he'd kept his mouth shut. She's his only real weakness, and there's an element of self-resentment at being so drawn to her, a rarely exposed vulnerability that manifests in his stomach each time their connection is shaken. Like a scolded child, he follows closely behind, no longer feeling like the bold adventurer, and knowing there's a strong possibility they are lost.

"Trouble ahead," Loren whispers. "Do you think I should go and check on her?" She picks the flower from her ear and takes another sniff.

"Probably best to let things cool down a little," Tom responds.

She nods and flashes a huge smile as she returns the flower. "Who are you going to tell first?"

"My mother, I think. She's been on at me for as long as I can remember. I'm sure she thinks I'm punching above my weight."

"Oh, you most definitely are!"

He smiles and gives her a gentle nudge. This conversation is what he needs to take his mind off things. "What about you?"

"I'll have to tell my other boyfriend first. Call things off now that we're official."

Tom clasps his arms around her and wrestles her to the ground. "Funny fucker, aren't you?"

"Tom, stop! Have you seen the size of the ants?"

He puts his teeth together and begins to hiss, occasionally slipping his tongue out. "It's the snakes you have to worry about, especially the anaconda."

She laughs and shakes her head. "Don't be coarse, Tom. You know it doesn't suit you."

They begin to kiss. "That flower smells so god damn good," he whispers. She brings his lips back to his, and they kiss harder, wrapping their tongues around each other's, their breathing quickening, pulses pounding against each other. Coming up for air, she puts a hand to her cheek. "I know; I can't stop sniffing it. It's intoxicating."

Tom closes his eyes and moves in again, his fingers hungrily digging into the layer of rotting leaves below, almost immediately brushing against something solid. He coils his fingers around the sharpness as he tongues Loren's neck, working his way up to her lips.

"Guys," Isla's voice floats across.

Once again, their lips lock with unusual urgency, tongues twirling around each other and teeth scraping, until they both finally release, gasping for air and giggling like lovestruck teenagers. Uncurling his fingers, Tom inspects the find—a hard grey shard decorated with a smattering of green. He runs his eyes over the patch of ground and finds two more fragments of what is undoubtedly animal bone.

Loren arches her body towards him. "Don't stop."

"Guys!" Isla's voice, sounding urgent but more distant than they both care for.

Tom pushes himself to his feet, extending a hand for Loren, who sticks out her bottom lip. "We better catch up," he says, running his eyes over the surrounding undergrowth, fragments of bone in abundance. He's no Columbo, but he knows death didn't come peacefully here, and the thought sends a shudder down his spine. "Hurry."

Loren adjusts her shirt and shrugs the backpack into place. "You okay?" she asks, scanning the trees ahead for a sign of their friends.

"Yeah, fine."

"Isla!" Loren shouts.

There's an uncomfortable pause that creates a prickle across Loren's skin. Momentarily, she realises just how vulnerable they are out here, and how much trust they are putting in Nathan to get them to a river that may or may not exist.

"We're over here, guys!"

Relieved to hear their friend's voice, Tom and Loren head towards the source, fighting against the clawing vegetation and taking more comfort at the sight of Nathan's backpack in the distance. Through the canopy, Tom can sense the sun beginning to dip, as though the forest has stolen more than its fair share of their time. He's getting more paranoid by the minute and will be glad to call it a day, marriage proposal in the bag.

They cover ground quickly, and Loren notices the trees surrounding them continue to become more intertwined, an orgy of limbs snaking in and out of each other, skin blackened as though horrifically burned. Only a smattering of leaves adorns the branches now, and some are without any foliage at all. Moans from all directions float across the forest as the warm breeze wraps around them. The forest appears to be suffering a slow death, taking what comfort it can.

"What's that smell?" Loren comments. It's faint but unmistakable, a heady cocktail of sweet perfume, creating a chain reaction of prickling skin and a stirring within. Her trepidation begins to ease, being replaced with an inexplicable yearning. For what, she doesn't know, but she's keen to find out. Tom follows in her footsteps, also drawn in by the heavenly scent carrying on the breeze.

As they catch up with Isla, she turns and smiles, stepping aside to reveal an explosion of colour—not just reds and yellows, but greens, blues, purples, and everything in between. It's a captivating display that seems out of place to Tom, a surreal and welcome sight when everything else around appears to be decaying. "Unreal," he mutters.

"It's the same flower we saw before," Isla says. "The smell; I've never known anything like it."

The flowers are undoubtedly the same variety as the one the strange-looking bee was hovering around. Tentacles reach out, exploring the air in front with colours so deep and rich they don't look real, all emphasised by the stark petals as white as snow against the dull grey vegetation beyond. They sway hypnotically as the warm breeze rushes across. Isla swears she can hear them emitting a low hum, assuming that's her interpretation of the projected vitality.

"Incredible," Loren remarks. "Christ, they look like they'll glow in the dark."

"Guys, this is great and all, but can we just get on with taking some pictures and then get moving?" Tom says. "Otherwise, we might get to find out if they glow in the dark."

Ignoring Tom's plea, Nathan steps towards the flowers, shrugging off his backpack. Tom is unable to resist. "Bzzz."

Without even turning around, Nathan flicks him the bird.

"Look after that good eye," Tom shouts, watching as the other two join him, releasing their backpacks and urgently scrambling towards the flowers. They ease themselves to the ground and lay down, basking in the vibrancy as if not a care in the world, each of them smiling and occasionally giggling as they take deep and frequent breaths of the surrounding air.

"Come on, guys, we really are running out of light. It will be so embarrassing if Jorge and co have to send out a search party!"

But they continue to bask, lethargically lounging in the large bed of rebellious flowers, stretching, rolling, all smiles and gentle laughter.

"Just a few minutes, Tom, please," Loren says. "Come over and join us."

"I really think we should be cracking on. It's going to be dark soon," Tom says sternly.

"I really think we should be cracking on. I'm going to bark soon," Isla mimics, sending the three of them into raucous laughter, hysterical and uncontrollable guffawing that grates down Tom's bones. He sighs, anxiously taking in the oppressive quiet around them. "Loren!"

"Don't be a killjoy. Come on, just for a few minutes." She pats at the ground next to her and winks.

Part of him wants to give in to temptation, but the rational side of him dictates it's time to move on. He's been dreaming about this day for so long—the forest, the proposal—but trepidation is creeping up on him now, and he's keen to outrun it before it takes hold. "Guys, come on; we don't want to be wandering around this place in the dark."

Even with the distant crackle of thunder, the three of them continue inhaling the flowers, moving from one to the next and letting out the occasional moan. Isla puts her hand behind Nathan's neck and draws him in, her other hand gliding up his leg.

"I see you two have made up then," Tom says. *Fuck's sake.*

Beginning to piss him off, he turns his attention away from them and grabs his phone from Nathan's backpack. He walks a few feet ahead to survey the terrain beyond the clearing, aiming the camera lens and taking a series of shots of nothing in particular. Still no sign of any river, just more trees. Blacker. Deader.

Something disturbs the vegetation ahead.

He holds his breath, eyes peeled, heart rate increasing as he draws closer. Half of him hopes his motion will send the source scampering off, but at the same time, he keeps the camera pointed ahead, thoughts of capturing something magnificent to show off to his friends, driving him forward. Slowing pace, he carefully moves the grasses aside and gradually lowers himself to the ground for better cover. Occasionally flicking off one of the inch-long ants that seem to be one of the few inhabitants of the area, he crawls across the soil, pausing as he spots a patch of moving fur between the leaves. Ignoring the sting on his left wrist, he gets the camera ready, his hand shaking with anticipation and more than a little fear. Behind him, he can hear the gentle moans of his friends.

"Guys," he whispers, knowing they'll not hear him but saying it for comfort anyway.

The movement ahead stops, and Tom freezes, thinking the game is up. He waits in silence, and the rustle of leaves commences, the accompanying grunting becoming more rhythmic and constant. *Stop shaking, you fool.* Dragging himself through the vegetation, ignoring the mosquitos that threaten from all directions, he moves aside the final thick stalk obscuring his view of the small clearing, immediately wishing he was rolling around in the colourful flowers with the rest.

The fuck?

One of the monkeys is wide-eyed, violently thrusting himself into the other, teeth bared and covered with what looks like fresh blood, some of it speckled across the hair and around the mouth. The other monkey is limp, brown fur matted with blood, black holes where the eyes should be.

Jesus fucking Christ.

Hairs bristling on the back of his neck, there's an overwhelming urge to get back to the group to tell them, but at the same time, he can't turn away. He takes a few shots as the excited primate continues its copulation with the corpse, its movements becoming even more frantic and aggressive, the grunting louder and more urgent. The monkey opens its mouth wider, showing the full extent of the longer and sharper teeth than the ones they saw earlier on. Suddenly it snaps its head around, launching into a tirade of raucous cries. Tom follows its stare to another monkey swinging from a low-hanging branch close by. The newcomer drops to the ground, and Tom listens to the approaching rustle, trying to steady the camera for the inevitable encounter.

Pausing its lunging, erection red and raw, the monkey arches its neck and begins sniffing at the air. Tom observes the ensuing stand-off, eyeing the visitor as it makes its way into the clearing, atmosphere uncomfortably taut, interspersed with the occasional shrill exchange of war cries. For a moment, nothing happens as they continue their warnings, sizing each other up, but finally, the visitor makes a move, and the two monkeys meet halfway in a frenzy of teeth and aggressive chatter. Tom watches, horrifically engrossed as the two primates roll across the floor, taking bites at each other and swinging their arms wildly, cries of pain and hostility ringing in his ears. It's a fierce display that he's seen on wildlife shows so many times, but close up, it's so violently real and graphic, each of the fighters now covered head to toe in blood, their fading cries difficult to listen to.

They're killing each other.

Finally, he stands, clapping his hands loudly, and the two monkeys turn to him, blood-stained teeth exposed. The expectation was for them both to scamper off, yet they continue to gaze towards him as though he's not a big enough threat and as though he has no right to call an end to their territorial display. A third monkey swings down from the branch above, and Tom decides they might be best left to it. He shrinks back into the flora and retreats towards the sounds of the moans.

As he turns and begins the short walk back to the group, a massive shriek explodes from a tree somewhere to his right. Startled, heart thumping, Tom comes to a stop, eyes falling across the eagle perched on the nearby branch. It's the size of a small child, head cocked, eyeing him as though he's a trespasser on its land, which he is. The bird offers another high-pitched scream as if demanding some form of explanation, and Tom slowly backs off, taking in the sheer size of the eagle's claws and beak. It's another encounter he could only have dreamt about a few days ago, but that now feels oddly sinister, the bird not taking its beady eyes off him. It shuffles forward along the branch towards him, and that's enough for Tom to continue his retreat.

What the hell is wrong with this place?

A long groan emerges from behind. "Guys!" Tom shouts. Another crackle of thunder from somewhere, slightly louder than the last. No response from the others.

He finally turns and begins pushing through the undergrowth, ducking and climbing over the spindly branches to the sounds of more moans, unmistakable exclamations of pleasure that are growing in intensity.

"What the—"

Shirts half-open, pants pulled down; their bodies writhe against each other. Nathan has one hand on Loren's crotch and the other on Isla's breast while his tongue hungrily searches for any flesh on offer. Loren has Nathan's dick firmly in hand and her lips wrapped around Isla's left nipple.

The eagle cries from behind.

"Loren!"

Obliviously, she continues to flick her tongue across the nipple and grip at Nathan's hardness.

"Stop it! Stop it now!" Tom screams, reaching for her wrist. She immediately begins to hiss, spitting and clawing at him in a way that reminds him of the animalistic scene just witnessed. Her nails scrape against his skin as he tries to drag her away, one hand still enveloping Isla's breast.

"Nathan!"

But there's no acknowledgement from his friend either, his face planted between Isla's legs, prompting more squeals of pleasure.

"Loren, please stop!" Tom cries, this time bringing an open palm angrily against the side of her face. The connection makes him wince, and he's immediately remorseful, but at least it gets her attention. Taking advantage, he begins to drag her away from the orgy. She kicks and screams in protest, maniacally biting at his wrists as though possessed, sending spittle spraying across his skin. Finally, with one huge heave, she's out of the clearing, and her thrashing begins to slow. She looks up towards him, face wrinkled in confusion, watery eyes suggesting some semblance of realisation. "I—I—what happened?" she asks, beginning to sob.

"Loren, what the fuck?"

It's all a blur; flashes of skin, the warmth of flesh. The smell, the music. "I—I can't—"

A loud shrill catches Tom's attention, and he snaps his head around to Nathan and Isla, their bodies intertwined among the flowers in a single glistening form, Nathan on top, aggressively pounding. Isla's legs are locked around his, her hands clawing into his buttocks and bringing him in even harder. Spilling down Nathan's neck is a stream of deep red, some of which spatters across Isla's cheek as he urgently continues driving into her. Offering a wild and unfiltered roar, Nathan yanks at Isla's hair, creating a harsh ripping sound. He holds the locks of brown above his head and lets out a maniacal laugh as Isla sticks out her tongue, catching some of the falling red rain.

Tom rushes across, grabbing hold of Nathan's shoulders. "Leave me alone," his best friend says through gritted teeth. Isla lunges as Tom continues trying to heave Nathan away, nails clawing across the back of his hand. She snarls and bites towards his wrist, but her teeth only scuff against hardness, not penetrating the flesh.

"Loren, help!" Tom screams, but she just continues to watch, mouth hanging open, eyes glazed, in a trance-like state.

It's in the air; he knows it, can feel it—a heaviness wrapping around him—thick fog developing in his brain. There's a sudden and irrational compulsion to let it take its course. Colours dance in front of him, the sweet smell once again concocting images of flesh and limbs twisting together, and an audible and comforting hum drifting across that—

The flowers! It's the fucking flowers!

Knowing he must make a move before it's too late, Tom holds his breath and pulls back on Nathan, but his efforts are futile as his friend lashes out, all fists and elbows. Isla lets out a snarl, her legs coiling tighter around Nathan, who smiles an inane grin, eyes watery and distant.

"Let him go, Isla. I don't want to hurt you!"

"Fuck off!" Growling, swiping her hand at the air in front, she catches Tom on the back of the leg this time. "He's mine!" A fresh stream of blood falls across the bridge of her nose as she plants her teeth into Nathan's chest. "Mine!" She begins lapping up the sticky redness trickling down his torso.

"Loren, for fuck's sake," Tom cries.

She turns towards the distant voice to see Tom's wide eyes, his face twisted in fear. Everything feels cloudy, almost unreal. She turns her attention back to her friends, still in the throes of sadistic and violent passion. Part of her just wants to nestle back into the bed of flowers, to feel their skin, bone, teeth against her, to taste the bitterness of their blood. But as she continues to watch the bizarre show, a disorienting wave of dizziness begins to wash over her, the forest becoming a blur of colour, voices slowing down, time coming to a standstill. She looks towards the ground and begins sinking into the brown softness.

"Loren!"

The voice is sharper this time.

"Loren, will you please fucking help me?"

The earth begins to release her.

"Loren!"

The fog begins to lift.

"Tom," she finally utters, a tear of confusion breaking free down her cheek. "I'm sorry." She makes her way across and begins working at freeing Nathan's legs.

"Hold your breath!" Tom commands.

Nathan begins kicking wildly at the air, an ankle catching Loren on the side of her head that immediately sets her ear ringing. "I'll fucking kill you!" he screams at them both, baring his teeth.

As Loren desperately clings to Nathan's left leg, Tom pulls back hard, and the bodies begin to separate. The uncoupling causes Nathan to let out a pained shrill, an animalistic howl that echoes across the forest. "Now!" Tom screams. "Grab his other one!" She does, and the pair finally begin to heave their friend away from the patch of flowers as he relentlessly spits and struggles against them. "Get the fuck off me!"

They're making progress; he's almost away from the clearing, but Isla lunges forward again, latching onto Nathan's legs. As Loren reaches for her hands, teeth sink into her wrist, causing her to cry out as the bolt of pain shoots up her right arm. "Fuck this!" Tom screams, instinctively bringing a foot into Isla's chest that sends her sprawling onto her back. She lets out a moan and, seemingly no longer concerned about the separation, begins pleasuring herself among the flowers.

Feeling a safe enough distance away, they ease Nathan to the ground, taking in huge mouthfuls of air as their friend claws desperately at the soil.

"What's going on, Tom?" Loren says, crumpling her forehead as she wipes a bloody wrist against her shirt.

"It's the flowers," he replies, panting, inspecting the scratches along his arms. "There's something in the flowers."

"What are you talking about?"

"Loren, a moment ago, you had your hand wrapped about my best friend's dick. What's your fucking theory?"

Her cheeks flush, and more tears begin to flow, Tom noticing the fresh droplet of diluted blood running towards her top lip. "Your nose— No, don't tilt it. Here, sit down. I'll get some tissues." He reaches into the backpack, fumbling around until he finds the box, while Loren puts her hand to her nose and inspects her fingers.

"I've never had a nosebleed in my life, Nath."

"Here," he says, gently dabbing at the streams now running from both nostrils. He glances across to Nathan, who has his face planted in the dirt, issuing an extended moan. "I think he's beginning to settle."

"I'm scared."

As Nathan goes to remove the flower with his other hand, Loren instinctively snaps her fingers around his wrist and furrows her brow. She stares at him intently for a second before finally releasing her grip.

"I want to go home," she whispers.

"Me too," Tom says, plucking the flower from behind her ear. Instinctively she tilts her head and inhales sharply, following the path of the powder as he launches the crushed flower over his right shoulder.

"It's the goddamn flowers, Loren," he tells her again, and this time, she nods.

"Isla, what the fuck are you doing?" Nathan cries from beneath them, trying to push himself up. "Ow, my fucking head!" His eyes dart frantically between his friend and the scene in the clearing. "Tom, what the hell is going on?"

"The flowers, Nath. We have to get out of here."

"What the fuck?" he utters, inspecting the open wound on his chest. "Isla!" he screams again, finally managing to push himself to his feet.

"This place isn't right," Tom says. "Please just get us out of here, Nath."

"We're lost," he finally admits, making his way towards Isla. "I'm sorry."

"Don't breathe in!" Tom shouts after him. The confession from his friend is unsurprising, but the words add elevated dread. Now they're relying on a drunken exchange in a pub to save them.

Emitting a high-pitched cry, Isla launches her assault on Nathan as soon as he comes within reach—limbs thrashing, head jerking erratically, teeth snapping at his flesh. Desperately, she brings a nail down his arm that instantly makes him recoil, but he retaliates by snatching a handful of her hair and dragging her away from the ring of colour. There's a huge feeling of guilt, but her twisted face only advertises hate and contempt, and the eyes, an unsettling vacancy. She claws at his arms, squealing and kicking like a scared animal, but finally concedes the fight and lets herself flop back onto the ground, taking in huge mouthfuls of air. "Fucking arsehole," she mutters between gasps.

"We have to go," Tom says, desperately rifling through his backpack.

Nathan shakes his head, looking towards Isla, who is muttering something inaudible, her fingers strumming against her side. "I'm sorry, guys," he mumbles. "I've really fucked this up."

"Here," Tom hands a bandage across from his small first aid kit. "This will have to do for now. Let's just get out of here, eh?"

"Which way? I have no idea which way we were heading or which way is back anymore," Nathan confesses. "Fuuuuucccccccck!" he screams into the blackened forest.

"I thought you could smell it?" Tom says, unable to contain the resentment for the situation they find themselves in.

His friend looks down to the ground, shoulders dropped. "I can't smell shit. I'm only going by what Jorge told me."

"Fucking Jorge," Loren says. "Why would you put our lives in the hands of a stranger, Nath? At what point, when you sobered up, did that still sound like a good plan?"

He shakes his head, not lifting his eyes from the ground. "I'm sorry. I've fucked us. I'm so sorry."

The three of them nervously scan the trees around, not even sure what they're looking for. Isla curls up into a ball, continuing to cuss at them under her breath as she claws at the ground.

"I'm sorry, too, Nath," Loren utters. "Look, we've got two hours before dark. We'd never make it back, even if we were certain of the way. I vote we continue. Nathan, you checked the map, saw the river. We can't be far away."

"It should be close." Nathan finally lifts his head. "Anywhere around here. We've not faltered off course; I'm sure of it."

"There," Loren says, giving a nod straight ahead. "That tree; it looks climbable. If we could get high enough, we might be able to see the river and the village. If there is one."

"You don't know shit!" Isla says. Continuing to sniff aggressively at the surrounding air, she alternates between laughing and hissing. "Don't know shit."

Loren looks towards Tom, eyes wide. "We've seen you climb."

He nods, knowing she would inevitably volunteer his services, but that's okay; there are very few things that he cannot scale, any tree, child's play for him. Since he can remember, he's been scaring his mum half to death, climbing trees, scrambling up rock faces, and that's only got more daring as the years have passed. Like father, like son.

"I'll do it," Nathan offers. "This is all my fault, after all."

Tom removes his shoes and socks and makes his way to the tree. "Stop being so pitiful, Nath. It doesn't suit you." Running his hand across the bark, he plans his first few moves, searching for the imperfections and indentations offering the lowest risk. He glances over his shoulder and nods towards Loren and Nathan. *You've got this, Tom.* Taking a deep breath, he coils his fingers around a small leafless branch and digs his toes into the first foothold. He hoists himself up, trying not to think about how high he needs to climb. Checking the branch above to see if it will hold his weight, it breaks off easily, and he turns, offering his friends a cautious smile.

Isla begins to cackle. "Whoops-a-daisy."

"Please be careful," Loren says.

"I will. Just hold onto her, and don't let her anywhere near the flowers again."

The branch to the right holds, and he's away, slowly testing each offshoot, committing and examining where his next foothold will be. It's slow going, but he's beginning to make progress. Limbs snap and crumble to the ground, but as he looks down, he guesses he's already about twenty feet high. *Focus, Tom.* Another moan from Isla has him hoping she is beginning to emerge from her intoxicating stupor, but her face suddenly twists, and she once again thrusts her hands between her legs and rolls across the ground. He's already experienced how strong it is, but this animalistic display sends a shudder down his spine.

As sweat drips down his forehead into his eyes, he tries to blink it away and get on with the business of climbing, the urgency of the dying light impossible to ignore. The ascent should be easy, but his fingers are becoming sore, as are his calves, and he curses himself for putting on the extra weight. His personality demands tunnel vision, though, and he's allowed the painting to take over—no room for anything else—hoping his focus and passion will result in something Loren can be proud of. The thought manifests itself into extra weight as he contemplates this and the responsibility sitting on his shoulders to find their way out.

Pausing the climb, he looks down, allowing his limbs to rest and the ache in his fingers to subside. Loren waves tentatively. Sitting on the ground, Nathan has his head in his hands. Isla writhes at his feet, her movements no less frantic. "This fucking place." Nathan came out of it so quickly, most likely his tolerance for drugs far greater than any of them. Loren, less so, but Isla appears completely lost.

A distant cry from the right catches his attention, the first sound he remembers hearing for some time not created by themselves, but it's one that offers no relief, pained and ominous. He scans the surrounding forest, eyes darting from one black branch to the next, but there's no sign of the source, no sign of anything.

Every limb aches as he continues navigating up the tree. "Come on." The proposal seems an age away now, a different time. They haven't even had the chance to enjoy it, suddenly thrown into desperation mode, the forest seemingly against them, conspiring to seal their fate within its black heart. Each movement grows more challenging as the responsibility continues to embed in his stomach. *How much further?* Even with minimal foliage, the gnarled deformity of this part of the forest makes it impossible to get a clear view. Above, perhaps another twenty feet higher, the branches seem to get thinner and open more freely as though celebrating their distance from the ground, from the darkness. They look contrastingly stronger, glossy limbs, some even sporting what looks like new growth that would be impossible to see from below through the deformed chaos. There's something to his right too. *A nest?*

From an uncomfortable distance below, he hears Nathan's voice mumbling something and what sounds like pleas from Isla, but he carries on, determined to get them out of this. A warm breeze blows across, and he waits for it to die before he coils his fingers around a small bump in the tree, heaving himself up. About four feet higher is the nest, wedged between a network of smaller branches. Just to its left is what looks to be a clear path to a sturdy branch and the promise of a prime viewing spot. He begins to make his way towards it, still unable to see clearly over the top of the canopy but getting close. If there's a river, he'll be able to see it soon. He moves again with urgency, the dwindling light impossible to ignore.

"I need it!" Isla screams from below. "It's not fair!"

Testing the branches in front by allowing some of his weight onto them, he finally begins edging himself towards the nest, holding the thicker limbs and surrounding vines for balance. Step by step, he makes solid progress, only pausing when the wind blows through. So close now. But just as he reaches for the next support, it breaks off in his hand, and he topples forward, flailing desperately for something to grab onto. More of the deceivingly brittle branches crumble in his fingers as momentum carries him forward, his right foot coming down hard on a neighbouring limb, prompting a long foreboding creak. He holds his breath and remains motionless, heart in his mouth, pulse pounding.

Another crack.

And another.

"Oh, shit." Finally, the branch beneath snaps, and together they begin their descent.

"Tom!" Loren cries from below.

His arms and back smash against a network of branches that crack and topple to the ground, but by blind luck, his fingers coil around a thicker and sturdier branch, and he manages to hold himself, leveraging his feet against the gnarled bark of the trunk. Immediate and intense pain explodes through his fingers and arms as he swallows air, countless feet above the ground, praying for this one to hold. "I've got this, Dad." Blood pounding in his ears, he looks down to see both Loren and Nathan with eyes on him, hands clasped around the back of their heads, while Isla fumbles in one of the backpacks behind them.

Face still twisted in fear, holding desperately onto the branch of the half-dead tree, he reaches for one of the thicker limbs and hoists himself up, scraping his legs against the bark, hoping to find leverage. Finally, he manages to wedge his foot between the trunk and another branch, and slowly and carefully, he begins working his way up again, his muscles screaming for mercy.

It's a strange and soft wail that emerges from behind, and as the frenzy of feathers comes to rest on the branch above, only inches from his face, Tom lets out his own little cry of surprise and tightens his grip.

It's the same type of eagle he saw before, perhaps even the same one, but it appears even larger as it sits above him, gloriously terrifying. Heart thumping against his ribs, Tom hugs the tree, not taking his eyes from the magnificent beast. The eagle eyes him warily for a few seconds before snapping its glance towards the other humans below.

No! No fucking way!

He's sure he must be wrong, trying to rationalise what he's seeing, perhaps the flowers again, some sort of hallucinogenic effect. But as he watches the huge bird strut towards the nest, talons efficiently wrapping around the branches, the object in its beak becomes even clearer. *There's just no way.* Bowing its head, the eagle releases the tooth into the nest. Human, Tom's sure of it. The gigantic bird offers one final look towards him before giving out a departing cry and efficiently navigating its enormous wings through the limbs of the forest, finally disappearing out of sight above the canopy.

This fucking place!

A breeze rattles through the bare branches, slightly cooler, but the ever-fading light cushions any relief. Feeling reasonably stable again, Tom cautiously makes his way up the next couple of branches, scanning the forest in case the eagle returns. Wedging himself between two of the thicker limbs of the tree, he balances on one leg, craning his neck toward the nest and peering into its contents. "Oh, Jesus." Nestled between the shells and half-eaten carcasses of offspring are countless human teeth, all shapes and sizes, some stained with blood, and some still adorned with fleshy paleness.

There's an immediate pain across his chest and an accompanying wave of nausea. His grip on the branches instinctively becomes even tighter. Unable to move, disoriented, all bravery gone AWOL, he looks down towards the others, and—

"Naaaathaaaaan!" he screams, unsure his words will even carry.

But it's too late, the knife sinking into the side of his best friend's neck.

He hears Loren's piercing scream and watches helplessly as she slowly backs away. Nathan drops to his knees, instinctively trying to plug the violent stream of red, the first bit of colour to dilute the forest green for some time. Behind him stands Isla, bloody knife in hand. Even from such a distance, Tom swears she's wearing a smile.

"Run, Loren!" Tom screams as she continues her slow retreat in obvious disbelief.

Isla brings the knife down again into Nathan's neck. And again, and again, chopping relentlessly while holding his head in place with a tuft of his hair.

"Run!" Tom screams again, his voice croaking as vocal cords strain.

Finally, Loren looks up towards him before taking off into the blackened trees.

Heart drumming evening more frantically, Tom urgently begins to scale the rest of the tree. He wants to go back and rescue his friend, but he knows by the time he gets down, there'll be nothing left to save. There's an urgency to get back to Loren, too, but he knows they need their way out. Letting out a scream of his own, a release of anger and grief, he throws caution out the window, moving swiftly from one branch to the next, not affording himself the luxury of testing each one, but praying they will hold.

Another five feet or so, he guesses he's approaching the three-quarter mark, but as he affords himself a look around, his climb is over. In the distance, just a few hundred metres ahead, he sees the sprawl of the village and the welcome return of lush green. Sheer luck that Loren ran in the direction she did. The river and the boats must be close, he thinks. Hope surges through him, and he immediately feels guilty for it. Everywhere he looks, though, there are more of those flowers; a shit load between him and—

The fuck?

He carefully brings himself further forward into the heart of the tree to get a better look. Even through the coiled branches and dimness, he can make out the pile of bones. From so far away, it's too difficult to say if they're human or not, but Tom's gut feeling causes him to let out a shudder. *And the teeth.*

Seeing something flash between the branches below, he begins the descent, trying to remain as calm as possible. He imagines Loren scrambling through the forest in the dying light, how terrified she must be, but he wills himself to be patient. One wrong move, it will all have been for nothing. As he works his way down, he notices Isla dragging Nathan back towards the patch of flowers. She appears to be talking in tongues now, a frantic and garbled explosion of nonsense only interrupted by the frequent sound of the blade sloshing against what's left of his friend.

Continuing to fight the instinctive urge for haste, Tom focusses on each branch, trying to recall which ones he used for the climb up. About twelve feet to go, he pauses to get his bearings and rest some more. Below, Isla still slashes away, covered head to toe in his friend's blood, smearing it across her face and bare skin. As she lets out a howl, face aimed towards the forest roof, Tom notices his friend's eyes are just black holes, and there's hardly a patch of his skin not covered in blood. There's a wildness to Isla that reminds him of the monkeys again, wide-eyed, governed only by violence and lust, no sign of humanity. Sadness and rage rush through him, but he forces himself on, all thoughts turning to Loren. As he navigates down the side of the trunk, he alternates his glance between the murderer and the skeletal limbs, finally sliding to the last branch and allowing himself to catch his breath.

A blood-curdling scream draws his attention back towards Isla. She's lying on her back, raising his best friend's head above her like a trophy, sprinkling the falling drops of blood across her breasts. Howling into the night, she brings the head down between her legs, letting out a repugnant moan that fills Tom with fear and disgust.

A subsequent cry prompts Isla to pause the debauchery, eyes darting in all directions, lips curled in a snarl. Tom recognises the shrillness, recoiling as another of the high-pitched shrieks rip through the forest. *The eagle.* He, too, begins scanning the surrounding trees until he finally observes the grey bird gliding in, wings outstretched and spanning at least six feet, no doubt hopeful of getting a share of the fresh meat on offer.

Biding his time, Tom watches as the bird circles above the small clearing, finally swooping in towards its target. In response, Isla stands, bringing Nathan's head close to her chest in an obvious claim of possession, snarling her warning towards the bird and waving the knife in front with her other hand. She swings at the eagle and screams as it draws close, but it quickly veers off, letting out its own less dramatic cry of frustration. Another eagle joins in, swooping across from the right, Isla flailing the knife towards it, teeth gritted together.

Tom takes his chance and jumps down, feeling his ankle give as his foot lands awkwardly on one of the protruding roots. He bites his tongue, resting for a moment against the tree to the sound of Isla's maniacal tirade and the surprisingly soft notes of the ever-growing numbers of birds. Only eagles, though. The only birds brave enough, or perhaps the only ones left around here.

He takes his opportunity, clumsily limping between the trees, eyes fixed on a nondescript patch of land, but one that will hopefully lead to the river. The knot in his stomach at leaving his friend tightens further, but grief will have to follow later. Loren's somewhere out there, and she's the priority right now. Blood pumping in his ears and ankle singing with pain; it's slow going, but hope keeps him going. If he can make it to the village, he can get help. The villagers will know the forest better than anyone. Perhaps Loren will find her way on her own. If not, they can come back for her.

As he flicks his gaze from the ground towards the black and twisted tree standing beyond his original landmark, undergrowth continues to slice at his legs, a reminder that he's at the forest's mercy. Doing his best to ignore the sweet scent of the flowers as it blows across and his peripheral vision full of mesmerizingly vivid colours, Tom keeps his eyes pinned ahead, running as fast as his legs can carry him. *That hum, though.* He covers his ears with his hands, internally singing the lyrics of one of his best friend's songs, trying to incite comforting memories, but the recent act of desecration brings a bloody curtain down on the show. So much blood.

Long grasses and spindly roots whip against his legs, but adrenaline fuels him. To his right, he spies another collection of disjointed bones, hardly any flesh on the grey, and impossible to tell what the animal once was. If indeed it was an animal. *They were goddamned human teeth, and you know it.* More remains to his left, slightly fresher, maggots writhing within what little flesh remains.

The forest continues to reach for him as he pushes forward, only now able to see a few yards ahead. Just in time, he ducks under a thick stray branch, momentum causing him to topple forward and almost lose his footing, the disorienting sight of yet further bones adding to his urgency.

Shadows from the moonlight cast an even eerier scene, a twisted boneyard of branches housing an even smaller graveyard within. Every creak of wood, every gust of wind, fills Tom with trepidation, and somewhere in the distance, he swears he sees movement between the trees. "Loren," he cries, pausing momentarily to get his breath back, willing for a response. Nothing. Everywhere he looks, limbs wrap around each other, reminding him of the sordid scene from the clearing—two sensible adults suddenly stripped of all dignity and thrusting themselves against each other so violently, beyond lust—something much more dangerous.

What was that?

Again, something in the distance; sounded like a howl of sorts. Human? Animal? God only knows. Just wanting out, he thrusts himself from the tree and continues his run, frantically scanning the area for life. The village appeared to be close when he was in the trees, but it feels like he's been running for ages, just more deceit offered by this hateful place. A snap of undergrowth to the right demands his attention, but the darkness only gives to more of those flowers in the distance, an explosion of luminous colour, much larger than the patches they saw before. The scent is strong, and he feels it seeping into him. The sudden heaviness it creates on his body and the mist he feels beginning to cloak his brain is impossible to ignore. Against the otherwise silence of the forest, he can still hear the gentle hum floating across, and momentarily there's that urge to give in to them again, to take what pleasure he can get from a forest that so far has only offered pain.

Get out of my fucking head!

Head down, trying not to breathe in as best he can, he continues weaving between the trees, but the breeze wraps around him, and that glorious perfume begins working its magic. More scenes from the hotel flash before him as fingers of vegetation continue to cut at his arms and legs. He suddenly feels dizzy—desire, confusion, exhaustion. Reaching an arm out, he comes to a stop against a tree, panting heavily, almost all out of fight. The smell, the music, the air itself feels as though it is layering around him, seeping through his cuts, spreading its poison through his veins. He wants to sit down and let it take him—to let it take his fear away, his guilt.

But as the breeze drops, he hears it, the trickle of water. *The river!*

His body feels leaden, but adrenaline once again begins to kick in, pushing the heaviness away and clearing the mist from his head. Straight ahead, like a series of luminous barriers, are dozens of clusters of those flowers, of every definable colour and more, and beyond those, he catches sight of a boat gently bobbing up and down.

Made it!

Even the thought churns his guts with guilt. He takes in his surroundings, observing the small puffs of powder leaving the flowers' pistils as a slightly stronger gust carries across. He watches the dust swirl above them in a hypnotically tornado-like fashion before simply dispersing into the night air.

Another howl emerges from behind, closer this time.

He sets off again, holding his breath, high on renewed hope and impervious to the pressure on his ankle. Not too far away, some moonlight fights its way onto the surface of the water, giving him a further boost.

There's a surreal aspect to the sight ahead to his right: torn clothes covered in dried blood, surrounded by a random assembly of bones, no skull to be seen. Thoughts turn to Loren once more as he fights the urge to gag, focussing on the silver glimmer ahead. *Come on!* Able to hear the wooden oar gently crashing against the side of the boat, he glances down as something connects with his right foot. More bones jut out of the soft black soil. They're everywhere. More flowers ahead, too, but he holds his breath and runs straight through, trampling them in the process. *Fuck you!*

He hopes that Loren managed to find a boat. He hopes there's a rational explanation for the decapitated human body he just passed. And he hopes the villagers will see them safely home. The explosion crackles across the forest, sending Tom to a crouching run, his heart in his throat. Face twisted in preparation for the inevitable bullet, he frantically darts in and out of the trees, scanning the surrounding dimness but seeing nothing. Confused, disoriented, vulnerable, he staggers forward, the fragility of hope obliterated as quickly as it had appeared.

Undergrowth tears at his arms and faces as he tries to stay hidden. He spies the ripple of water again between the two trees ahead, but patches of those fucking flowers are everywhere. Inhaling deeply, he emerges from his temporary cover and starts his sprint, ducking and weaving through darker terrain that only presents itself from a few feet away. To his right, wood splinters, and the crisp gunfire deceitfully surrounds him, sending a foreboding shudder down his spine as he ducks down even further, veering to the right and scrambling across uneven ground.

Another explosion pierces the air, Tom feeling the impact of what he thinks must be tree bark falling across him. He continues his run, head down, but the delayed onset of pain surging across his left shoulder sends him sprawling ungracefully to the ground towards a patch of colour he was so desperate to avoid. He falls on his right side, but as he rolls onto his back, the unbearable wave of agony swells across his body, and he notices the red stain spreading quickly across his shirt.

It's over.

Screwing his eyes shut and clenching his teeth, he stifles a cry.

Colours surround him, and he watches the powder float majestically through the air as another waft of warmth blows across. From somewhere out there, behind the veil of darkness, he can hear voices closing in, but the pain is too much, and he remains on his back, staring at the rays of moonlight somehow puncturing the impossibly thick canopy. The rustle of undergrowth from somewhere close draws his attention, but not enough for him to try and move. This patch of ground feels comforting, a cool blanket wrapping around him and taking away his pain. And the humming is beguiling, an angelic chorus that seems to be lifting him towards the moon and causing his body to tingle with excitement.

The pain begins to fade, his skin becoming a hyperactive composition of nerve endings that prickle with excitement, and the knot in his stomach is no longer—replaced with a stirring, a yearning for Loren's flesh that feels wrong, but at the same time so right. All thoughts for her safety fade, and now he's lost, only thinking about her skin, her lips, her—

A voice floats across, momentarily disturbing his train of thought. Another sharp inhale, though, and he's back to the previous night, his mind filling with snippets of their carnal acts, ones that had always lurked in the back of his mind, but he was always too shy to try. He feels himself getting hard and begins to encourage it, stroking along his length and letting out small moans of pleasure. Imagery flows thick and fast, but he's insatiable. Every lustful thought he's ever had invades his head, all merging into a single erotic montage that begins to manifest across his body. It's as though he can feel every touch, every breath wrapping around him, providing a cocoon of humid warmth. Hands and faces of ex-lovers join with those he lusts after in a single orgy of pleasure. He can smell their hair, taste the saltiness of their flesh, feel their moistness against him. Waves of pleasure ripple across his body, creating a euphoria he hopes will never end.

The flowers themselves seem to dance around him in the breeze, and he basks in their glorious glow, a light show of vast proportions against the bleakness of the canopy. Over the gentle and hypnotic harmony in his head, Tom hears the tranquil sound of running water that prompts a fleeting memory, something about a river. But that can wait now. This is where he wants to be.

More voices, even closer now. And laughter.

Tom begins to laugh with them, poking at the myriad of blurry colours dancing in front of his eyes. Footsteps. He can hear footsteps. He laughs harder, continuing to rub himself, lost somewhere between reality and utopia—a limbo without pain, a vacuum of pleasure, elevating him towards a never-ending crescendo of ecstasy. Above him, blurry faces come into view, and slowly, the fog fades to reveal yellow crooked teeth and dark eyes animated by the rhythmic movement of the flowers. *Jorge.*

"Fucking tourists," the voice swims across—dreamlike—deep and in slow motion.

"Can't handle it, Jorge. Too much for them," the other one says. "Throwing their fucking money around like kings and fucking queens! Stupid English fools."

Jorge leans over, grabbing hold of Tom's legs. "Nature can be an evil mistress, my friend; beautiful but lethal." Tom tries to resist, planting his fingers into the earth, but the other man grabs his wrists and assists in dragging him a few feet away from the flowers. "She draws you in with her irresistible perfume," Jorge continues, "and then works her dark magic. Soon, you can never get enough."

Jorge leans back against a tree, crushing and sprinkling one of the flowers into the half-filled rolling paper. He licks the edge and ignites the end with the familiar cigarette lighter, NJ etched on its front. Nathan Jacobs.

"Moderation, my friend," he says.

Momentarily, Tom pictures his best friend's decapitated head, joint hanging from the corner of his mouth, and an uncontrollable fit of hysterics washes over him, explosive and unfiltered laughter that hurts his throat. Even as Jorge leans forward, resting the cold steel of a blade against his neck, he can't stop cackling. "Smoking's bad for your health," he says, sending him into another fit.

"Where are the girls?" Jorge utters, applying pressure with the blade.

"She hates being called a girl," Tom says, inducing more uncontrollable laughter. He swears he just saw something move between the trees.

Jorge begins to laugh too, pressing the blade further against Tom's throat until a small stream of blood begins to work its way down. "If you tell me, I'll make it quick. Otherwise, I'll tear off your skin, piece by—"

A blood-curdling howl echoes across the forest.

Tom twists his neck against the blade of the knife, just in time to see Isla's head come to rest only a few inches away, her face still drawn in a maniacal expression, the glow from the flowers filling her eyes with false life.

"Strike!" Tom screams.

Tom watches Jorge snap his head towards the trees, the man's mouth falling open, but only a rasp emerging. He can see shadows moving, hear the ground crackling from all around, and suddenly Jorge's face is melting, running down in a series of dark streaks reminding him of the long rainy car journeys in the back of his parent's car. Noting the blade now emerging from Jorge's neck, Tom manages to raise both arms as the man crumples towards him, the exposed dull grey sharpness missing his right eye by only inches. Wheezing and rasping, Jorge continues spitting out threats in native and English tongue, snarling his contempt at Tom, who continues clasping at the man's shoulders, wincing as the foreigner's blood spills across his face.

As Jorge's spasming body slows to a twitch and then to nothing, calm is only temporary, another ear-splitting gunshot crackling through the air, accompanied by a piercing and agony-filled cry sounding far from human. Tom's scared to move an inch, his limbs rigid with fear and heaviness. Around him, the night is filled with snarls, panting, tearing of flesh, and as he continues emerging from the spell cast by nature's perfume, the pain in his shoulder explodes down his left-hand side once again. Still cowardly hiding under Jorge's lifeless body, he blinks away the blood leaking into his eyes, fearful of whatever it was that emerged from the darkness. Above him, there's another bout of pained screams, and Tom holds his breath as he hears more crackling of the forest carpet.

And silence.

Light but heavily tainted air rushes pleasantly across Tom's face, and he takes the opportunity to inhale its sweetness, watching as more of the powder spirals into the night air and as the luminous flowers hypnotically sway just out of reach. Once again, the pain begins to subside, and this time, a wave of tranquillity washes over him. His fear, anxiety, and guilt give way to a comforting peacefulness that once again elevates him from the ground towards the kaleidoscope of warm colours swimming between the skeletal branches of the trees.

And he wants more.

As he tries to roll back towards the centre of the patch, someone grabs his hand and begins to pull. "No, I don't want to leave," he screams.

His calmness has gone, a feeling of intense anger beginning to course through his body. "Fuck off!" he screams, kicking his legs and flailing his arms. "Just fuck off!" As he digs his fingers into the ground, desperate for another hit, the colours begin to fade, as does the enchanting scent that he knows he's becoming enslaved to. And the humming, that beautiful humming, begins to sound cruelly distant. "Who are you? I'll fucking kill you!" he screams.

Only a soft whimpering emerges from above as he claws against the coarseness of the forest floor. "I said I'll fucking kill you!" He lashes out, his leg connecting with something hard that sets him free once more. *Need it; nothing else matters.* Dragging himself desperately against the soil, sniffing madly at the air like a dog, he closes in on that wonderful limbo once again, but just as he breaks through, he feels the grip on his ankle again. "Leave me the fuck alone, won't you," he cries, continuing to lash out with overflowing rage.

More whimpering from above, as though from an injured animal, and from further out, more voices. Tom kicks out again, prompting another cry of pain followed by a roar and—

*

"Fuck."

As soon as Tom tries to move his left arm, it roars with pain. He slowly opens his eyes, wincing as pain explodes across the front of his head, his watery vision allowing only a blurry view of the riverbank as it passes by on his right. Another gunshot explodes from somewhere far away, and he ducks instinctively. And then another, followed by the faint sound of cheers and laughter.

He lifts his right hand, tenderly circling a finger over the brutal stinging across his face, and it all begins coming back to him. Peering over the back of the boat, he observes the village fading into the distance, but not quickly enough for his liking. "Fuck you, Jorge." It's as he reaches for the oar that he notices the engagement ring slipped across the little finger of his left hand.

"Loren."

His entire body begins to shake, the tears finally coming, raw and explosive —for Loren, for his friends, for the guilt.

The boat violently rocks as he smashes his fists against its side, letting out his own unfiltered series of howls until he eventually crumples into a ball, exhausted, hardly able to keep his eyes open. He knows he will take the guilt to his grave, that the forest—his choice—will forever haunt him. Praying that nobody follows and for the nightmare to end so he can at least begin to grieve, he watches the stars above slowly pass in the clear night sky. It's the morning he longs for now—enough of the darkness.

*

Squinting into the early morning sun and seeing no sign of the village behind, Tom begins to cry, more dampened than before, more controlled. This selfish relief to be alive, he hates himself for. "I'm so sorry, Loren." Ahead, impossible to tell how far away, he can just make out the silhouette of another village, no signs of the mysterious flowers along the banks.

Loren saved him; he knows it. Even in her drug-induced state, bleeding and fighting temptation, she somehow managed to drag him onto this boat and set him free.

How is he supposed to tell the families? How many other tourists have perished in that forest at the mercy of the locals? How is he supposed to get through this, manage the guilt, the inevitable nightmares? How can he go on without her?

He can't find it at first and begins to panic, but as he stretches his fingers deeper into his pockets, relief kicks in as they brush against the smoothness of the pod.

Just in moderation. Just enough to get me through.

THE MASTERPIECE

They're words.
Just words.

TOM PLACES HIS laptop into the drawer of the mahogany desk and gently pushes it closed.

Today is a new day.

Eyeing the machine on his desk, light from the window diluting its blackness, he thinks back to the day he stumbled upon it in the grimy window of the antique store. It was purely by accident, an impromptu drive to get away from the house. And the wife.

He'd never seen the store before but had been overjoyed to make the discovery. Full of old easels, pens, cameras, and all sorts of other seductive objets d'art, it was the old Smith Corona that made the hairs bristle on the back of his neck. He knew it had to be his as soon as he saw it. He even gave it a name, right there and then.

Today is a new day.

He's seen a few over the years, but nothing compared to this, with its slick black sheen and undeniable aura of importance. Without even knowing the price, he'd taken the label to the counter and told the guy he wanted it. Strange man, hair as black as the machine itself, small dark smudge across his right cheek. Almost choking at how cheap the guy was selling it, Tom couldn't wait to shake the guy's hand. All in cash, as dictated in the shop window. The man even gave it a fresh polish and threw in some beautiful paper; told him that it was the best you could get. Tom laughed out loud when the man said the machine came with the guarantee of a masterpiece.

Today is a new day.

Since that day, 'Black Beauty' has sat on his antique desk next to the lounge bay window. There was never any intention to use it; that would be too much like hard work. Tom thought its presence alone might be enough to inspire him, to end his drought of productivity.

Alas, no such luck.

Early this morning, he decided it was time to change tactics. He will write the first few pages on the machine just to get him started.

Today is a new day.

Sniffing at the air sneaking through the slightly ajar window, he pulls the chair further in towards the desk. The familiar sounds of buzzing traffic and muted conversation bring an energy that excites him.

He winces as he knocks back the cold dregs of coffee, clears his throat, and gives his fingers a loud crack. Magic is about to happen. Hands hovering over the keys, he lets his mind go blank—an empty vessel ready to be filled with mystery and adventure, tempestuous tales of protagonists with imperfect pasts, and a redemption arc that nobody sees coming.

Come on, Black Beauty!

Fragments of forced and terrible ideas begin to invade his mind, quickly disappearing without a trace. It's only a matter of time, though— patiently panning for that small nugget of gold. As he sits, staring intently at the keys, seconds become minutes. The vein in his neck starts to throb in perfect synchronisation with each impossibly loud tick from the large wall clock. His legs begin to tap frantically under the desk. The buzz of life from beyond the window that usually inspires starts to feel more like a taunt, and soon the familiar and bitter taste of self-doubt and self-loathing begin to work their darkness. He glances at the clock once more to find an hour has already passed.

His fingers begin to hammer the keys:

i

am

fucked

In two hours, she will be home, and he'll have to feed her lies again. Just once, he wants to be able to share real excitement. A mid-life crisis, that's what people called it when he told them he was taking a year off to write a book. Some even studied him with a confused, almost pitiful look, as though he had just told them he was having a mental breakdown.

He's not sure of the truth anymore.

Tom gets up and paces the room, mumbling more of his mantras without conviction.

Fiona was supportive early on. They had savings behind them, enough for a few months—but the judgmental looks have started to creep in.

Must write something. Must write something.

As he takes his place once again in front of Black Beauty, he begins to question if he's got it in him. Selling a handful of short stories is a different beast from writing a novel.

Come on! Think, you idiot!

He walks over to the cabinet, letting his hand linger over the hatch as if he might have the willpower or self-control to deny himself a drink. *Just one*, he thinks, pulling it open. Bypassing the glass, he grabs the neck of the bottle and takes two generous mouthfuls.

With further mutterings of self-abuse, he performs two more laps of the room and sits back at the desk, shoulders slumping, all the markings of defeat written across his face.

"Fuck this for a game of soldiers."

Forty-five minutes before she's home. His body is rigid with anxiety. He knows there's little chance of productivity in such a state. Too much pressure. *One more drink.* He shuffles to the cabinet and swigs back another generous mouthful. Shaking himself off, he takes his seat once more, fingers poised, determined not to concede another wasted day.

Tick-tock.

He writes a few words of uninspired drivel and immediately rips the paper out, tossing it in the bin under the desk.

She will give him that look. He'll have to go back to work. Back to real estate. Back to Hell.

Visualise, Tom, visualise. Start somewhere, any-fucking-where.

Less than thirty minutes to go, he returns to the drinks cabinet. *Last one.* Two mouthfuls. He rushes back to the desk.

Just write something; anything.

Fingers crashing down again: YousuckTom

He finally admits defeat, warily getting to his feet and giving Black Beauty the one-fingered salute. The room begins to spin, catching him by surprise, and he reaches for the edge of the desk to steady himself, trying to recall the number of whiskies consumed.

Mouthwash.

He dashes upstairs but catches his foot on the third step, not quite throwing his hands out in time and paying for it with a tooth through his top lip. *Fuck!* He scrambles to his feet and runs to the bathroom cabinet, desperately reaching for the green bottle as if it was antivenom.

Gravel crunches, causing random prickles across his skin and a feeling of his stomach dropping out. *Shit! Shit! Shit!*

The liquid is foul, but he gargles with intensity and spits it into the bowl. His reflection is unflattering, dark circles under the eyes and grey skin, the inevitable result of sleepless nights and countless days indoors pacing the living room carpet.

And he remembers the words he typed. If she sees—

With the palm of his right hand skimming the banister, he begins skipping down the steps. Noticing her approach through the frosted glass, he jumps from the fifth, ungraciously landing with a thud and an explosion of pain in his ankle. *Fuck!* He unfolds, pressing his hands against the wall for leverage and thrusting himself into the lounge, adeptly ripping the paper from Black Beauty and grimacing as he launches himself onto the couch, heart thumping wildly.

The door opens, revealing deep caverns of angst etched into her forehead. He knows she's had a bad day. "Hey love, how was your day?" he offers anyway, and rather too jovially.

"Rotten! Yours?" she replies with an accusatory frown. "What happened to your lip?"

Instinctively, he puts his hand to his mouth. "Shaving. Stray hair."

"I hope you've written more than that," she says, nodding to the piece of paper in his hands.

"Oh yes, twenty-three pages today, Fi. It's really starting to come together. You sit down, love, and I'll bring you a nice cup of tea," he utters, in all too familiar survival mode. Holding the paper close to his chest, he makes his way to the kitchen.

"Did you pick up my dry cleaning?" she asks.

Shit. Shit. Shit. "I was going to, Fi, but I was on a roll; couldn't stop typing. So much good stuff!"

"Tom! I told you I'm going out for lunch with the bigwigs tomorrow. It's a big deal!"

"Sorry, love, just got carried away. You have loads of nice dresses, though!"

She lets out a half-growl, half-sigh. "I don't ask for much."

"I know, I know. I'm sorry, love," he replies, wincing at his self-loathing tone. His knuckles turn white as he grabs hold of the kitchen bench and stifles a scream. He wants to make it. He wants to be successful, but there's too much pressure—the lies, the anxiety. He just wants to be left alone. How can he be expected to focus, come up with magic if all he's surrounded by is—

Written below his previous rants are twenty-eight letters. It's a skill he's developed; the ability to quantify the number of letters in a word or sentence. It helps bring back some control when things seem to be slipping away.

itwouldbeeasierwithouthertom

Time stands still as he studies the crumpled bit of paper on the counter, mouth slightly ajar.

"Where's that cup of tea?"

The kitchen seems to be getting smaller, closing in as if there's a sudden lack of breathable oxygen. He rushes towards the door, swinging it open and vomiting over Fiona's geraniums. *You're a drunk, a fucking loser.* "Coming, love," he finally replies, wiping the fluid from the corners of his mouth with a tea towel.

Tom checks the paper once more. No change. A knot begins to manifest in his stomach, one he knows is only just making itself at home.

He didn't write it. He's sure he didn't write it. Even after the whisky, he can't imagine himself ever writing anything like that. It's a thought that has crossed his mind, that's for sure—more than once if truth be told—but there's no way he would put it to paper. Would he?

No liquor tomorrow.

He crumples the paper and throws it into the kitchen bin.

The night continues like any other, aside from the familiar and all-consuming anxiety eating away at Tom. Forced into the corner of the couch, her legs cutting off his circulation, he rubs her feet, thinking about the precious minutes of writing time slipping away, watching the abominable displays of egotism from camera-hungry narcissists.

He could be in front of Black Beauty right now, creating a masterpiece.

Yes, Tom, go ahead and tell yourself that.

Did he write those words—a whisky-induced rant? Is he cracking up?

Relief kicks in when she finally calls it a night and disappears to the bathroom to apply her creams.

Tomorrow is a new day.

But then he remembers. Today is Thursday. Sex night.

Their weekly session is, without fail, uninvolved and uninspiring. It's the same every week—a bit of lacklustre foreplay, followed by the missionary position, accompanied by the bed's gratingly rhythmic and mechanical squeaking. Without fail, she almost always orgasms, but he can't claim it; all he can do is try and time his climax with hers to avoid further awkwardness.

Tonight, it's going worse than usual. Her face projects something worse than disappointment, but even with his flaccid member redundantly thrashing inside her, she stubbornly battles through, albeit to a less than mediocre orgasm. He withdraws apologetically and watches her place the vibrator on the bedside table before turning over without so much as a goodnight.

There will be a struggle to get any sleep tonight; he knows it. Fiona will be snoring in five minutes, and there's no way he's going to beat that countdown. He just waits, trying not to think about anything.

And she's away.

He carefully swings his legs out of bed and tiptoes across the bedroom carpet. His excitement begins to build as he takes the stairs two at a time, being careful to miss the seventh one that always emits an impossibly loud creak. As he approaches the living room light, the glare from the streetlight outside is enough to bring his attention to the sheet of paper in the typewriter. His finger hovers over the light switch, delaying the inevitable, but he finally takes a deep breath and flicks it on. Heart thumping, he moves slowly towards Black Beauty on less than solid legs, observing the lines of text written across the uncreased paper

admititthinkofalltheextratimenoquestionsnopressure

There's no delay this time. The new line, written underneath the previous ones, induces heart-pounding anxiety and a feeling of weightlessness that forces Tom to double over. A million theories rush through his head, but none of them are plausible. Was it him? Another childish rant?

Perhaps she wrote it?

No, she didn't get the chance. Besides, I screwed it up and threw it in the bin.

Am I losing my fucking mind?

Remaining in the position for a while with palms pressed against his kneecaps, he waits for the black floaters to dissipate and for the feeling of weightlessness to pass. Finally, he slowly gets to his feet and removes the paper from the carriage. He rips it up, first into halves, then quarters, carrying on until the pieces are too small to tear. Eyeing the forever seductive drinks cabinet in the corner, he considers a tipple to help alleviate unease. Instead, he defiantly walks to the kitchen, discarding the remnants of the paper in the bin and returning to bed.

*

The day comes and goes without any flashes of brilliance—only distraction and whisky—but at least no menacing messages from the machine. His anxiety levels show no sign of letting up, as he considers it's already the end of the week, and he still hasn't written anything new. He can't go back, though, not to that—interminable boredom and stress. But his mind is consumed by the fact that today is Friday, which means dinner out with her awful friends, an unbearable evening of superficial conversation that always cements his lack of faith in humanity. What car are you driving? Who are you wearing? Where are you holidaying? Who are you fucking?

Fuck them all.

*

"So, Tom, how's the writing going? Are we going to see the movie soon?" Richard asks.

Tom eyes the clueless prick before taking another swig from his glass. "Working on it. Genius doesn't happen overnight, though."

In the background, he hears a snigger from Fiona that induces a wry smile from Richard.

"What's it about, Tom? Can we have a clue?" Richard persists.

"It's about the hopelessness of humanity," Tom replies, unsmiling.

The waiter comes over with the main course, inadvertently breaking some tension.

"How's the new car, Richard? Looks sweet!" Gary says enthusiastically.

"Oh, don't start him off on the car, Gary. It's his new love; it's all he talks about at work," Yvonne responds.

But Richard begins giving everyone the low down—the speeds it can reach, the people he's left at traffic lights, the looks he gets from women. He's in his element, centre of attention, and Fiona is lapping up every word.

Tom excuses himself and pulls a seat at the bar. Nursing his drink, he watches the table continue their rabble about things, places, and people he doesn't care for. He observes Fiona as she frequently glances towards Richard with almost childish awe. Her body language is different, too— exaggerated—and she keeps flicking her hair and pulling at the lobe of her ear. Even her laughter sounds off. It feels surreal to him, watching the person he spends so much time with behaving so strangely. It could be the drink, but he suspects there might be more to it.

He orders another, taking comfort in the clink of the ice cubes as he swirls the golden liquid around. Occasionally, he looks back at the table to find some of them looking over in his direction and laughing. But could that be paranoia? He's not sure of anything anymore.

Thank God, he thinks, as he finally hears the slaking of chairs behind.

As they say their goodbyes, Tom catches Richard whispering something into Fiona's ear. He doesn't say anything in the taxi, though. Neither of them offers a sound as they make their way through the fake hopefulness of the neon night, back to slow and uncomfortable suburbia. He notices her face is already changing. The frown is returning, and the sparkle from her eyes is fading. Youthful enthusiasm has all but vanished, and as they roll up outside the house, she's just plain old Fi once again. She throws off her shoes and stumbles up to bed, all part of the Friday night routine. In a few minutes, she'll be snoring again, and Tom will be lying next to her, wide-eyed and waiting for an idea that will never come. The subsequent weekend will be full of resentment from both sides and a nagging itch that Tom will be unable to scratch.

Deciding he's not ready for the onslaught of normality, he takes off his shoes and makes his way towards the drinks cabinet for a nightcap. On his way, he catches sight of the typewriter from peripheral vision but refuses to acknowledge it this time. *There's just no fucking way.* He opens the cabinet, grabs the bottle of scotch by the neck, and affords himself two generous mouthfuls. There's no satisfying burn, just an ominous feeling things are going to get worse, much worse. Unable to ignore it any longer, he turns towards Black Beauty and warily makes his approach.

Two lines beneath the others, on paper that was torn to shreds the previous day.

Dickandfisittinginatree

Shesfuckinghimtomfuckinghisbrainsout

The same disregard for grammar and punctuation is impossible to ignore even as the familiar feelings of confusion and disorientation wash over him. Only hours ago, this piece of paper had been ripped to shreds and binned. Now it sits in the carriage with alleged reports of his wife's infidelity.

What the fuck. I'm going Jack fucking Torrance here.

Tom stares at the paper, reading the text repeatedly as if it might provide a clue or explanation. He feels too present, too aware, to put it down to losing his mind. The paper's weighty feel as he pulls it out adds further tangibility to the fact something else is going on.

Something quite impossible.

He makes his way to the kitchen, this time opening the corner cupboard and reaching for the matches. He grabs one from the box and lights it only on the second attempt, his fingers trembling with urgency and unease. Marching across to the kitchen sink, Tom observes the words of torment disappearing as the yellow flame hungrily consumes the tainted paper.

Tomorrow he will take Black Beauty back to the shop. His decision is made. Maybe the strange man knows something or can give him information about the previous owner, something to go on perhaps. It's a long shot, but what has he got to lose aside from looking like a fool?

Tom settles into the couch and stares towards Black Beauty for as long as his eyes will allow.

*

His head feels like it's on fire as he squints into the morning light.

manoramousetom

A new line is written across the paper he recently set on fire.

"This isn't fucking funny!"

He rips the paper from the carriage and carries it through to the kitchen, wincing with each move. *No liquor today.* He throws it in the bin and takes a large step back, as though its heavy and sinister connotation may manifest itself into something even worse.

"Tom!"

Am I losing it?

As he continues stepping back, he crosses into the lounge, but the hammer of the typewriter's keys stops him dead in his tracks. It's a short sharp burst, but one that leaves him shaking, the contrastingly joyful ding from the carriage sending a shudder down his spine.

Slowly, he glances over his shoulder, eyeing the sheet of paper that once again mockingly teases him.

sortherouttom

"Tom! What's all the noise?"

Another sharp burst of letters followed by the ominous ding: *youreafuckingmousetomafuckingservant*

Oh, fuck! Fuck!

He snatches at the paper, stuffing it into his pants pocket.

"Tom!"

"I'm coming, goddamn it!" he shouts in reply.

As he walks through the hallway, teeth digging into his lip so hard he can taste blood, Tom feels unhinged, as if he's not in control. He hears the hammer of keys behind but continues up the stairs, past wedding photographs lining the walls depicting happier times.

Fiona's still in bed, nursing her head. "Would you be a darling and get me some tablets, please?"

"Are you fucking him?"

Her brow furrows, and the immediate crevice across her forehead splits it in two. He knows the look. She's preparing for battle—and she usually wins. "Fucking who? What are you talking about, Tom?"

"King Dick! Are you fucking him?"

"Have you lost your mind, Tom? We're both married. We're not sixteen. I'm with you, and he's with Laura. You know that! What's got into you?"

"You've done it before. I've seen the signs!"

Fiona pushes herself up into a stronger position. She's on the offensive now. Battle lines are being drawn. "Are you going to hold that against me for the rest of my life? I was young, stupid, and drunk. Everyone makes mistakes! I thought we were over all of this. What is all this, Tom? What's the real issue here?"

"What did he whisper in your ear?"

"When?"

"Last night. I saw him say something as we were leaving."

"Christ, Tom, this is ridiculous. He just said that it was nice to see me, that's all. He meant as a friend." She strengthens her position further. He knows she's going in for the kill. "Is it the book? Self-doubt again?"

It stings immediately, sucking the wind from his sails. He perches at the end of the bed, a lump in his throat, pressure developing behind his eyes. He bites harder into his lip, but it does no good; the tears begin, and in a matter of seconds, he's consumed with familiar feelings of self-hatred and the emasculation of failure.

"Tom, I've tried my best to accommodate this mid-life crisis, but look what it's doing to you. To us. Perhaps it's time you moved on, got back to work?"

Her words fill him with endless sadness. The thought of going back to that place is more than he can bear. *What is happening to me?*

"You spend too much time alone, Tom. Your head is so full of fantasy you're losing your grip on reality. Honestly, I think it's time to call it a day. You gave it your best shot, Tom."

There's a weight to her words that falls heavy on his shoulders, a crushing honesty that makes it difficult to breathe. Anger is long gone, replaced with a child-like fragility. He looks towards her, but the returning look of pity pouring from her eyes is of little consolation.

"Besides, we're running through our savings far too quickly, Tom."

It's over. I've failed.

She shuffles across to him, placing a hand on his cheek. "So, you'll ring the office on Monday?"

He puts his head into her neck and reluctantly mumbles a "yes."

They stay like that for a while, Fiona stroking the back of his head tenderly. "Any chance of those tablets now, silly?" she whispers.

"Sure."

"Tom," she utters, just as he gets to the door.

"Yes, dear."

"I'm meeting Felice later for coffee. She and John are going through a few things, that's why she wasn't there last night. But how about we go for lunch later—the Italian in the square perhaps?"

Tom nods and forces a smile. "Sounds nice, dear."

There's no sharp intake of breath or churning of the stomach as he reaches the bottom of the stairs, noticing the paper in the carriage. He simply lets out a sigh. It's just how it is now. Solemnly, he walks over to the typewriter to read its latest appraisal.

schmucklaughingstockpussy

Tom dutifully checks his pockets. Of course, impossibly empty.

He angrily rips the paper from Black Beauty. "Just popping out, love," he shouts, grabbing his jacket from the rack in the hallway. An array of emotion spirals through his head as he carries Black Beauty towards the car: relief to be getting it away from the house, but primarily disappointment that it didn't provide the inspiration he was looking for. *A masterpiece or your money back.* It's the end of a dream, a failed escape from boredom and mediocrity.

It's the end of a story that never truly started.

He thumbs the address into his phone and heads off. Even after all its taunting, Tom has immense respect for the beast in the back. In the rearview mirror, it glistens magnificently in the morning sun, suggesting a level of prestige that he just couldn't live up to. Perhaps it's just waiting for a talented enough author, someone who can conjure a true masterpiece. Maybe then, the respect will be mutual.

Denver Street, here we go. Just a bit further down. But there's something very different about the place, something making his skin tighten. He rolls the car to a stop as he approaches the end of the street. Turning it around, he slowly drives back. No sign of the emporium, though, as if it never existed at all, the street boasting only derelict houses decorated with graffiti and furnished with boards across the windows.

No way.

He sits in the car for a while, pondering what is happening to him. Questions run through his head in no particular order, and he has answers for none of them. What does he do with the typewriter now? Is Fiona lying? Does he just concede failure? How can he possibly face going to work?

Eventually, he starts the engine and drives—no destination in mind, just an urge to stay away from the house for as long as possible. In the distance, a neon sign catches his attention: *Liquor.* His thirst is immediate and overriding. He pulls up at the shop, and as soon as he enters, feels self-judgment kicking in, but purchases a bottle of scotch, nevertheless.

Sitting back behind the wheel nursing the bottle, he catches sight of Black Beauty in the rearview mirror, loaded and ready to go. Once again, the paper is flawlessly erect and home to the same messages of torment, plus one more line. He turns to look at the latest offering: *shesatitrightnowtom*

Tom urgently unscrews the lid and takes in some of the liquid. *Fucking thing.*

Decision made; he screws the cap on and starts the drive towards the tip. The typewriter has only brought him more grief; perhaps this will at least allow him to move on from such—

As if on cue, the familiar hammering of the keys begins again.

Don't look, Tom. Just drive.

He can see the carriage moving in the mirror, and it takes everything he has to resist the urge to stop. *Nearly there.*

Finally, after what seems like an eternity, he pulls inside the gates and parks next to one of the large half-full metal bins.

Ignore it, Tom! Ignore it!

Hand on the door handle, he lets out a sigh as he turns his head, giving in to the inevitable moment of weakness and curiosity.

adelphihotel

The knot in his stomach reminds him of its residence. He taps the address into his phone with shaking fingers and wheel skids out the gates. Houses pass, traffic lights change as he drifts in and out of autopilot, his mind consumed by confusion, jealousy, and rage. He wants it to be a lie, for all of this to be some twisted manifestation of crippling paranoia and self-doubt. Two streets away—people on the corner chatting and laughing—*are they in on it too?*

Just as the hotel comes into view, the keys hammer down again in another short torrent of madness. He resists the urge to look, focussing on the building ahead: The Adelphi—missing the E on the sign, perhaps thirty storeys high—brown, depressing, and more than a little seedy. He parks the car and glances back at Black Beauty: *roomd46.*

Making his way to the entrance, he finds no security waiting at the gate and not a soul behind the reception desk. He's no idea of his intentions but begins to sprint urgently up the stairs, momentarily wondering why boy wonder would bring her to such a place and why Fiona would accept such a rendezvous. But then it clicks—no chance of bumping into a familiar face—the perfect place for such a sordid affair.

There it is, D46. Discreetly looking up and down the corridor, and with nobody else in sight, he tiptoes across, placing his ear against the door. Muffled laughs and muted voices stir more anger. He knows the door is inevitably going to be locked.

He grabs his phone from his pocket and slinks away to the corner of the corridor. There's no grand plan here. Nearly twenty minutes pass before the elevator pings, and after what seems like an eternity, a young couple finally steps out, looking as though they haven't a care in the world. Frantically, Tom begins tapping at his phone keys. They eye him warily, sniggering as they unlock the door to a room on the opposite side.

Five more minutes pass, and he hears the click of a door.

Heart pumping, taking in rapid breaths of stale air, he shuffles nervously against the wall. Voices. Louder this time. He knows it's Fiona, even before he sees her. And dickhead. They step out of the room—one last kiss—and now she is off towards the stairs.

Tom gives it five minutes and follows her. A small part of him wants to lie down and concede, let the world do its worst, but another, the part that makes him slam his fist into the wall on the way down, wants so much more.

Black Beauty. So sturdy and reliable. How can he possibly get rid of it now, when all it has done is provide him with truths?

He doesn't need her; all she has done is distract and let him down. How is he supposed to concentrate on the job at hand? It's time to move on. As he swings the doors of the hotel open, cool fresh air rolls over him, and it's a welcome relief from the staleness of the makeshift brothel. He marches to the car, his mind continuing to play out all possible scenarios, but there's one that keeps haunting him. Without her, he can write all the time, just him and Black Beauty.

There's magic in that machine, and he just needs to find a way to channel it. *Imagine what we can achieve together.*

Wedontneedhertom is the new message on the paper.

"Damn right!"

He sinks more of the golden liquid and performs another extended wheel skid to the sound of hammering keys. He turns, just as the movement of the carriage comes to an end: *shewontgoeasilytom*

The raucous beep of a horn gets his attention, and he swivels around, dragging the steering wheel to the right just in time to avoid the oncoming truck. *Fuck!* Taking another few swigs of whisky en route to calm his nerves, he rehearses the imminent confrontation.

She won't get out of this one.

He pulls up the driveway behind Fiona's car and takes two more mouthfuls for courage. Carefully and affectionately, he carries Black Beauty from the back seat and places it back into its rightful place on the desk in the lounge. "Home sweet home."

Upstairs, he hears the thrum of the fan in the bathroom. She's singing. *Fucking singing!* He strokes his fingers affectionately across the top row of keys before dropping into the couch, shifting uncomfortably from one position to the next, a mixture of nerves and excitement, stiffening at the eventual familiar squeak of the seventh step.

Confrontation has never been his strong point; he buckles too easily. It's the story of their marriage. He can see it so clearly now, how one-sided it's been. All this time, he thought he was the weak link—neglectful, too caught up in his dreams of becoming a writer—everything his fault. But he's been brainwashed. She just wanted him to feel weak; vulnerable. But no more. She's been caught red-handed this time, and she can't get out of this one.

"Hi, love. I didn't hear you come in," she says, rubbing her hair with the towel, the whiteness of the dressing gown casting a contrasting innocence.

"Just got in. How was coffee?"

"Haven't been yet. Just got out of bed; having a bit of a lazy day," she chirps.

Her face is hidden behind the towel. *She can't hide forever.*

"Funny. I swear I just saw your car about ten minutes ago."

"It can't have been me, darling," she replies, drying her hair with now impressive ferocity.

Heart racing and stomach churning, Tom digs his fingers into his legs, trying to keep a lid on his rage.

"I saw you, Fi. With him."

She finally stops drying her hair, letting the towel fall away.

He studies her features, the initial and immediate defensive hardening and tightening of the forehead, giving way to a resigned softness and vulnerability that suits her much more. As her face visibly relaxes, her eyes begin to glisten, and her shoulders drop. She falls back into the chair with a long deep sigh. Wiping a fresh tear away, she looks up towards Tom.

Spill it, dear.

Her gaze continues towards him for what seems like an eternity until she finally leans forward in the chair and says, "I'm sorry, Tom. I just feel so—so lonely. He pays me attention. Makes me feel special. Important. I feel like I've lost you—to the writing. Even when you're not sitting at that bloody desk, you're always away in fantasy land. You're not here with me. Not present."

"How could you possibly feel important at that shitty hotel? And is that all it takes? A bit of attention for you to spread your legs. After ten years of marriage?" He tries to remain calm; composed. She's too good at the switch, turning things around on him. She does it all the time.

"It helps, Tom," she snaps, shedding more tears.

"For fuck's sake, Fi. I rub your feet, cook your food; I'm like a servant tending to your every need. What more do you want from me?"

"I want you to want to be here with me, to talk to me, interact as other couples do. You're always so obsessed with your stories. I may as well not exist! I just want to feel loved, Tom."

She becomes hysterical, sobbing, head buried into her hands and shoulders heaving. Tom doesn't recall her ever looking as fragile.

Oh, well done, Fi.

Rage begins to subside again into confusion and inevitable self-hatred. He knows she's right, though; that's the problem. He's given her up for his only true love—writing, storytelling. The lump in his throat is back, and he digs his fingers further into his legs to keep his own tears at bay.

"So, what now?" Tom asks. He was ready for a full-blown argument—words they would regret and all sorts of slander and abuse, but so far, it's been a tame affair of truths and admissions.

"You have to choose," she says, slaking an arm across her face. "It's me or the writing, Tom. I refuse to be second choice anymore."

"You can't make me choose, Fi. This is my passion. Without this, I'm just—I'm just—"

"You were happy, Tom. Once. We were happy! You've been at this for two years now, but all we have to show for it is a wrecked marriage and a big hole in our savings! We agreed a year at the most, but nothing is happening, Tom. I'm sorry. I know it's a bitter pill to swallow, but it just might be that you're not good enough!"

Her words crush him. They're words he has internalised many times, but from someone else, someone that's supposed to love him, they go deeper and hurt more—a finger in an open wound. "Maybe if you had just let me get on with it and occasionally lifted your fucking finger around the house, it would have been different," he says. "Maybe if you didn't insist on trying to change me so fucking much, I might have it in my heart to love you!"

Fiona's eyes widen, and her mouth drops. Tom's not sure if it is surprise or fear; it's a new look, but one that provides him with a surprising amount of satisfaction.

"Tom, I'm the one with the job, earning money so you can live in—"

Black Beauty's keys begin to hammer in the background, snapping both their heads towards the typewriter. The thundering noise ceases abruptly, giving way to an ominous silence.

Ding!

More words begin to thunder from Tom's faithful machine. Another ding, another short burst.

And silence.

Fiona turns back to Tom. "What the—"

"I'm doing this for us. For a better life! Can't you see that? So you don't have to work anymore at that shitty job!"

"How is that possible?" she finally says, beginning her walk towards Black Beauty.

"Fi!"

"What's going on, Tom?" she asks, reaching towards the paper.

"Fi, don't!"

She leans in towards the machine, reading each of the lines. "I don't understand. We don't need her, Tom. What does that mean? And who's we? And—"

There's nothing to hide now. It's all out there. He walks over to her side and reads the three newly created messages.

sheslyingagaintom

theywilllaughandfuck

andlaughsomemore

"Tom, what is this?"

He opens his mouth, but Black Beauty has said it all.

Keys thump against the paper, and together, they watch the words form:

letswriteyourmasterpiecetom

Ding!

onlyoneendingheretom

Ding!

killhertom

"What the fuck, Tom!" Fiona mutters, slowly backing away towards the door.

"Fi, let's just talk about this."

"Stay away from me."

Ding!

wecantlethergotom

Ding!

shesseentoomuchtom

Switching focus between Tom and the typewriter, Fiona reaches blindly behind for the handle.

gethertom!

His head spinning like a centrifuge, it's the bad thoughts coming out on top, and after all, Black Beauty has only served him well, been straight with him all the way, unlike anyone else.

Besides, they have a masterpiece to write.

As she finally coils her fingers around the handle, he rushes towards her, slamming her against the wall so hard the mirror crashes to the floor and splinters glass around them. Her eyes wide with surprise, she claws her nails down the side of his face and lets out a loud and piercing scream that catches Tom by surprise. A movie scream he never thought was real. High on adrenaline, events suddenly feeling surreal, as though he's watching from above, he knocks her flailing arms away and slides his right hand across her mouth. The muffled pleas are no easier to bear. She kicks her legs out in desperation, sending fragments of glass sliding across the floor, but he has his other arm wrapped around her throat and easily drags her off balance.

"Shh," he whispers.

She manages to get a hand on the door frame, but he kicks it away easily. Nothing from Black Beauty; he has this anyway. They're in the living room now, her legs kicking helplessly and aimlessly at the air until he finally heaves her across the couch.

Breathing heavily, face carved with lines of terror, she screams again. He makes to hit her—a threat to try and get her to shut up—but the scream continues. *It's the fucking weekend.* And just before his fist connects with her face, there's a look of disbelief in her eyes that will stay with him until they put him in the ground. She slumps back against the upholstery and slowly slides down until her bloody mouth comes to rest on the arm of the couch. A garbled moan escapes her as she tries ineffectually to push herself up.

He pauses, hearing her words in his head: "you are not good enough."

All the lies, all the deceit—like butter wouldn't melt.

He can hear keys tapping in his head but no movement from Black Beauty. He's writing his own story now. He's the one in control, and it's got to be one hell of an ending. She reaches out towards him, tears rolling down her face into the damp fabric beneath.

"I'm sorry, Fi. This was how it was meant to be. This is my story."

He reaches across to the desk, heaving Black Beauty into his arms. There's no going back now; he knows what he must do. He lifts the typewriter into the air and holds it there for a while, in position, watching as his wife manages to raise herself slightly on the journey to regain some composure.

You've crossed the line, Tom.

He scrutinizes her movement, each failed attempt, each mini success. He observes her features, the hope and despair projecting from her eyes, and it turns his stomach with grief and sadness. But this is work now; this is research. Well past the point of return, this is good material—depth for the story. She finally manages to lift her head towards him and eyes the machine held high above his head like a trophy. He studies the fear and realisation in her face, making a note to detail the way her adrenaline appears to surge, her moves suddenly stronger and more deliberate, as though survival instinct is reanimating her. She thrusts herself up, but her arms suddenly give way, and she's back to vulnerability.

"Pl—"

Before she can raise her arms, he brings the typewriter down onto her head, gravity doing most of the work. There's a dull thud, followed by another garbled moan. As he lifts the machine to observe the damage, he notes the misshapen nose and the dark blood beginning to pool. He directs a dry retch towards the carpet.

She's still alive.

He brings it down again, raises it, down again, raises it, down again— "Will you just fucking die?"—and suddenly he's in a frenzy, veins popping from aching arms and bloody saliva rolling down his chin. Somewhere in the fit of rage, he's sure he hears her skull crack. Even as her struggles cease, Tom continues the relentless pounding until his efforts are accompanied only by a horrific sloshing noise. There's a moment of disbelief, a feeling of dream-like detachment again that sends his head spinning and the room closing in.

But as he finally takes a step back, a sudden and painful twinge down his spine snapping him fully back into reality again, he begins to sob like a child.

I've just killed my wife.

He lets out a small yelp, wincing as he leans across and lifts the machine from the wasteland that was once his wife's head. The paper is unblemished aside from those menacing lines of text.

As he places Black Beauty back on the desk, its glossiness helps grief pass quicker than could ever be expected, his skin already prickling with excitement at the thought of writing his story. No disturbances now, no breaking of focus. With a spring in his step, Tom walks through to the kitchen and puts the kettle on. Shuffling from foot to foot, he puts a teaspoon of coffee into the cup and begins to whistle. There's a bird on the fence outside; it warily cocks its head and returns his stare.

"I've just killed my wife."

The bird flies off, uninterested in his confession.

The click of the kettle startles him, and he fills his cup and returns to the living room, sloshing some over the brim onto the floor. But there's nobody to tell him off anymore. It's just him and Black Beauty. And—

There's no longer a mark on it. No blood, no skin, no bone. Nothing. It's as good as new.

From the pocket of Fiona's pants, the familiar sound of a text message sounds. *Miss you already. How are you?* No name, just a number.

"She's been better."

He walks quickly through the house, drawing curtains and pulling down blinds on the way—making sure all the windows and doors are locked. He cannot be disturbed. Finally, he sits down to write his story.

With fresh paper in the carriage, he begins to type everything just as it happened. The words come quickly and easily, and this time it's his fingers hammering the keys into the thick and luxurious paper. He gets up only when he must, for the toilet or a glass of water. He doesn't eat, doesn't wash—but he's on a roll.

The house phone rings, the mail is delivered, and the world goes on around him. Someone knocks at the door, but he doesn't get up. It's a fucking masterpiece, no time for breaks. He doesn't even notice the smell that's starting to develop, so lost is he in a familiar world of betrayal, revenge, and magic.

Flies start to circle him, occasionally landing on the white paper. Tom flails and roars in disgust. Pages pile up, but Tom is relentless. He knows it's a race against time. He pushes through the pain, hands like claws, and two days straight without sleep. How could he possibly sleep with this story inside him? The phone starts to ring more frequently, and there's another knock at the door. Someone's shouting, too. But Tom is in the zone, at one with Black Beauty, and they're a million miles away on a fantastical journey together.

So close to the end now. How many days have gone by? He lives the emotion of the story, the tears, the laughter, the grief, and the ultimate freedom to write the fucking thing. More knocks at the door, this time more frantic and urgent. Louder voices. Someone's calling his name. The pain in his shoulders and neck is now crippling, but he carries on—words in his head that must make it to paper.

"Nearly finished. Nearly finished," he chants to himself.

Fingers thrashing away, his nerve endings sing with pain. *Come on.*

He hears glass shatter—possibly the front door. *So close now.*

Voices louder and sharper, he hears the click of the door.

Wait.

The first cop enters the room, young and nervous, gun shaking towards Tom. "Step away from the desk, hands above your head!" he orders.

"So close, just a few seconds," he mumbles.

"Do it now," the cop shouts, trying to steady his hands. It's all he can do to not vomit on the spot.

Tom continues to write, muttering under his breath with every stroke. "Just let me finish—last few lines!"

Another cop enters the room, older, carrying himself in the way only those with years of experience can. "What the hell is going on?" he says to his pale-faced colleague.

"This guy. He's fucking crazy," the kid replies.

"Nearly done, guys!"

The second cop begins his approach. "Don't make me make you!"

"One more minute," Tom pleads.

"There's no fucking paper in the machine, punk!" the veteran cop screams.

And as Tom plunges his fingers down for the last few times, he watches with disbelief and confusion as the key hammers into only the blackness of the ribbon.

Into oblivion.

"No! No, that's not possible!"

Grabbing him roughly by the shoulders, the cop hoists him from the chair.

"No! That's not right. I've just written my fucking masterpiece!"

His hands are quickly cuffed, and the cop marches him towards the door.

"People have got to see my work!" Tom screams. "It's fucking genius!"

"Shut up!" the cop says, forcing him into the back of the car. The younger one gets in the passenger seat, still white as a sheet.

"You get all sorts of weirdos in this job, son," the older one says as he starts the engine and pulls away.

Rocking back and forth, Tom stares out the window, no longer sure of anything. He recognizes some people from the street, eyeing him as though he was some sort of circus freak.

What have I done?

Each street of the car journey brings its own set of buildings and people. Sounds of laughter and shouting; stories to be told, but not for him, not anymore.

He spots something in the distance. The sign. The emporium!

"That's it! That's the place where I got Black Beauty," he cries. "You must listen! There's something not right—something—"

"I won't tell you again. Shut it!" the older one says.

"But—"

"Shut it!"

As they get closer to the store, Tom sees a figure standing outside, the jet-black hair a dead giveaway.

Traffic lights change to red.

As the store owner starts walking towards the car, Tom presses his face against the window, observing the bundle in the man's right hand.

Paper? Pages?

"Look, he knows—the guy with the black hair—he's going to tell you everything! He's got my book, see!"

"It's your last warning, you crazy bastard!" the old one screams.

Why can't they see him?

Only inches away from the rear window now, the owner winks at Tom, peeling off the first page and thrusting it towards the glass.

As soon as he saw the old Smith Corona, he knew it had to be his. He'd seen a few over the years, but nothing compared to this one, with its slick black sheen and undeniable aura of importance.

"Guys—look, he's right here, standing next to the fucking car. That's my book! Why won't you fucking listen?"

The younger one turns his head and casts a glance out the window to satisfy Tom's request. "There's no one there, man."

"Fucking crazies! Probably get off by pleading insanity," the older one says.

Tom turns his attention back to the owner once more, observing the manic smile stretching across his face. He watches him let go of the first page, and as the paper impossibly begins a journey upwards towards the clouds, not even a rustle from the nearby trees. The owner releases the second page, the next, and then the lot, each sheet taking off on its unique path.

"It was a masterpiece!" the black-haired man shouts through the window.

The traffic lights turn green, and they slowly move away. Tom slinks back into the chair, watching his manuscript dissipate in front of his very eyes. Such a bittersweet ending.

He smiles, knowing he had it in him.

My masterpiece.

*

The store owner checks himself in the antique mirror on the wall, sighing as he eyes the small stream of ink running down his left cheek. "Goddamn it!" he mumbles.

He lifts his fringe to reveal the three sixes etched into his scalp, deep wells of ink bubbling and swirling with ferocious intensity. It always happens when he gets over-excited, and boy, does he have a good feeling about Gerald.

It takes two plastic cups to collect all the overspill, and he places both on his desk and out of sight. He'll use the ink to soak more ribbon later.

The store owner knows Gerald will be home by now and begins hopping from foot to foot with glee. Nice guy, very well-mannered, good dresser, too. The trilby might have been overkill. He couldn't wait to get the typewriter in the back of his car. Twenty dollars short, but it's never about the money.

Whistling cheerfully and very out of tune, the store owner skips to the back of the store. *There's my beauty.* He stretches across the other treasures and grabs the shiny red Smith Corona, carrying it over to the counter. The ribbon is fresh, already loaded with his special ink.

Oh, how exciting.

He sprays the antique mirror with the liquid from the green bottle and smears it carefully across the surface. A strange little noise leaves his lips as he rubs his hands together, accompanied by an excited shiver down his spine. His master loved the last one, thought it up there with the best, but something tells him this story will be the true masterpiece. He excitedly loads the red Corona with a fresh sheet of special paper.

In the mirror, he observes the inside of Gerald's living room—*comfy but drab*. Already loaded with paper, the typewriter sits on top of a large wooden dining table, underneath a rather nice and expensive-looking chandelier.

He watches and waits.

Finally, Gerald pulls a chair up and relaxes into it. He sits there for a while, looking thoughtful, occasionally lifting his fingers above the keys and dropping them back down to his side again. Distraction stage two kicks in as he scratches the back of his neck and runs his hands through his thinning hair multiple times.

Trilby makes sense now, the owner thinks.

There's a voice from somewhere else in the house.

"One minute!" Gerald shouts.

This time, the voice is louder and sharper, and the store owner watches the woman stomp into the room with her hands on her hips, eyebrows forming the shape of a seagull mid-flight. "Gerald, have you taken the dog for a walk yet?"

"Oh, you are going to be a lot of fun," the storeowner utters.

Gerald brings his fingers back over the typewriter and frowns. As his wife marches out the room in disgust, muttering something under her breath, his fingers finally come down hard towards the keyboard, and the keys from both typewriters begin to hammer simultaneously into the paper.

bitch.

The store owner smiles and once again rubs his hands together as he watches Gerald roughly grabbing the paper and disappearing out of the room. Softly but purposefully, he begins to type something on the red Corona; again, both sets of keys doing their stuff.

It's started, the man with the jet-black hair thinks to himself.

He thinks of himself merely as the director. The mirror gives him some material, and he provides the prompts, but the characters write themselves, each one different, with their own demons and scale of emotions. *Best job in the world!*

ABOUT THE AUTHOR

MARK TOWSE is an Englishman living in Australia. He would sell his soul to the devil or anyone buying if it meant he could write full-time. Alas, he left it very late to begin this journey, penning his first story since primary school at the ripe old age of 45. Since then, he's been published in *Flash Fiction Magazine*, *The Dread Machine*, *Cosmic Horror*, *Suspense Magazine*, *ParABnormal*, *Raconteur*, and many other excellent mags.

Mark's work has also appeared on many exceptional podcasts such as *No Sleep*, *Creepy*, *Chilling Tales for Dark Nights*, *Tales to Terrify*, and *The Grey Rooms*, to name a few.'

2021 saw the release of his debut novellas, 'Nana' and 'Hope Wharf,' and early 2022 saw his recent novella 'Crows' take flight.